The Porlock Maria

Chris Gladstone

Cover illustration by Chris Gladstone and Andy Gladstone
Original ship image by Ben Salter

ABOUT THE AUTHOR

Chris Gladstone moved to Porlock, Exmoor, in 2012, where he runs a bed and breakfast with his wife Clare. His previous publications include a local history book and also 'Court & Dagger' published in 2022, a dramatic and comic story in verse based loosely on 'Lorna Doone', the Exmoor classic novel by R. D. Blackmore.

Dedicated to those inspirational people of Porlock Vale and Exmoor who selflessly donate so much of their time, energy and kindness to the benefit of others and to enrich the lives of everyone who dwells in this wonderful and uplifting corner of our land.

The wise man does not lay up treasure. The more he expends on others, the more he gains for himself. The more he gives to others, the more he has for his own.

Lao Tzu

The Porlock Maria

Prologue

The snow swirled and whipped horizontally across the bleak white ruggedness of Exmoor. Sheep huddled, faces down and eyes closed against the sting of the cutting wind as the bitter evening turned into yet another stark night. The distant black plantations gradually faded into the darkness until the only light that could be seen came from the ancient farmhouse perched at the top of a combe, standing solid and safe in the rugged wilderness.

Inside, the dogs were settled near the cosiness of the hearth. From the kitchen, the old lady, a warm shawl around her shoulders, brought out a tray.

'Here you are children, here's your hot chocolate. Now sit down by the fire and stay warm. It's very wintry out there tonight and there's an icy wind blowing.'

The old man settled back in his faded armchair with a large whisky. His two young grandchildren, in slippers and dressing gowns, sat on the hearthrug by the resting dog in front of the warming log fire as, outside, the wind whistled around the old cottage, sending the occasional gust down the chimney to puff wisps of smoke gently into the room. The girl, with a little cough, wafted one away.

'You know,' said the old man, smiling, 'when I was young and I did that, my mother would tell me that those little clouds of smoke were small ghosts, coming in from their frozen worlds outside to enjoy an evening with the living, to remember briefly what life was like. They're harmless, she said, so we should let them be. They'll disappear again soon.'

'Do ghosts really exist, Grandad?' asked the little boy in wonder.

'Oh, yes, they're very real,' replied the old man, peering at the wide-eyed children through his glasses. 'You may not see them but they are around us all the time. They're in the walls of our houses, in the floors beneath our feet, in the stones on the moors, in the old wood of the roofs, wandering among us all the time. They usually stay hidden as their time in the light has passed but sometimes,

1

occasionally, they like to come back to see their families and loved ones. Most are quiet and happy but some, just a few, are not. Probably just like the children at your school.'

'Are the unhappy ghosts the ones that try to scare us?' asked the little girl.

'Yes, but you shouldn't be scared if you meet them. They're just grumpy and can't hurt you.'

The fire crackled and spat and the dogs stirred briefly before settling again.

'Can you tell us a ghost story, Grandad?' asked the little boy eagerly.

The old man put down his glass on the table next to him and picked up a small inscribed wooden box that lay there. He opened it slowly and took a long look inside. He closed it quietly, looked up at the children, his eyes glinting in the firelight. He smiled and began his tale.

1

The Somerset village of Porlock nestles beneath the north edge of Exmoor on land that curves gently down to the distant sea. Set within the wide expanse of lowland settlements known as Porlock Vale, the village itself dates back to Domesday times and earlier, a place where old traditions linger long in its quietness of thatched cottages, restful tearooms, winding alleys and enticing shops. A popular place for tourists, some cherish the impression of time stood still, of old values so rare in this twenty-first century world, of strong friendships and solid community. In the heart of the village stands the parish church that has witnessed and honoured the lives and deaths of countless generations. On this mild September day, it had been full again.

The congregation had moved slowly and sombrely from the church to The Castle Hotel close by. Propping up the bar, the three retired men sipped their IPAs, all fidgeting with their black ties that felt awkward and constrained. Bob the Box, ex-undertaker and former harbour master at nearby Porlock Weir, was the oldest - stout, grey-haired and with a ruggedness borne from generations of hardiness across the moor and the coast. Next to him stood Vince, tall, stocky and whiskered, still shrewd after a working lifetime as an urban copper, retired to the village almost twenty years previously. And Bill, ex-banker, well-dressed and handsome despite an increasing paunch, keenly perceptive and increasingly mellow after retiring from city life more recently. Despite the differing backgrounds, all three men had become close friends, enjoying their retirements on Exmoor and occasionally involving themselves in more boisterous activities and adventures whenever the mood took them. Yet today, they were quiet, all lost in thought despite the murmurs around from family and loyal friends who gathered there on this sorrowful day.

Old Rik was gone. The service had been brief, a few apt words said by those who knew him, those who'd been there through his life, who'd seen his business grow and flourish, making him a wealthy man, a good man loved by all. And now he's gone, just shy of eighty. One moment happily signing one last deal, and then all was ended in a flash - literally.

'I can't believe he went that way,' said Bill, mirroring the thoughts of the others. 'I mean, what are the chances? Standing on deck at Bristol right next to the crate, pen in hand, signing off the paperwork, probably planning a beer or two at The Prow to celebrate a new life of retired bliss. What did the docker hear, according to the papers? A fizz, then pop, then BOOM! And that was it for poor old Rik. Bonkers.' Bob took another measured sip. 'He was a kind and generous man. He was in a dangerous trade but he knew the risks. Very careful, always was, but accidents happen.'

'Yup,' said Vince, 'I know what you mean. When I was in the force, we dealt with everything - old guns, bombs left over from the wars or smuggled in from God knows where. Accidents often happened. Poor old Rik. What was it, an old grenade not deactivated properly?'

'Seems so,' said Bill. 'The verdict was clear – just an accident. Though from the mutterings I hear, some believe another tale.'

Around the room, the milling throng of seventy guests or so, in muted and respectful clothes, had split into a range of groups, from distant cousins to local friends, from youngsters to the seated old. The buffet table almost bare and glasses never empty, Rik's closest family did the rounds, his son Victor the host. And soon enough, the mood improved as, small talk done, everyone relaxed, making friends, telling jokes, remembering Rik, his cheeky smile, his open soul and his warmth.

All spoke of Rik Williams, the local boy done good. Born in Porlock, Exmoor-bred, he was a country boy who started off with close to nothing when times were hard. He tried to make a living there but, frustrated with his lot, he joined the navy, saw the world and survived it with a smile. Then, the Cold War at an end, Rik felt another pull and, by using contacts and working fast, a new career was born. Army surplus, excess gear, and his business quickly grew into a multi-million-pound trade across the continents. Despite the darker underside, Rik always played it straight, a tough yet honest trusted dealer who won respect from all. He travelled far and loved his work but his soul was bound to Exmoor so he moved back home and, with his wife Jane, he bought a small estate.

Bill, Vince and Bob, three rounds in, surveyed the busy room, seeing faces from the moor and some from distant lands. All Rik's family, from near and far, had come to pay their respects, to be there at this solemn time to see the old man off. As his mother had died some years ago, eldest son Victor now ran the show and, with his wife and children, would carry on and run the estate as best they could, as Rik had always planned. The family was well renowned as honest, true and fair, who gave employment when they could to local tradesmen, youngsters and any who wanted work, always paying well and, in the pub, generous to a fault. All were there, a kindly gathering of sorrow and contemplation.

Through the rolling hum of the room, the sharp 'clink clink' of a glass could be heard and 'Quiet!' from various voices. When chats had reduced to whispers, Vic, a tall and elegant man in his black tailored suit, stood at one end as the crowd gave him space.

'I'll keep this brief, you'll be glad to know,' he said amidst tender smiles. A few words of thanks, a mild joke or two and 'Dad would have loved this,' then Vic stood up straight and came to the point.

'It's hit us hard, all of us. We're all close friends here and, when something like this happens, we all feel the pain. Rikard – Rik – Dad was a wonderful father, friend, businessman and colleague without an enemy in the world. His death was a tragic accident, whatever some may believe, but he'd had a full and happy life and, I'm sure, no regrets. The only regret he may have had is not to see the fruition of his brain-child, the first Porlock Triathlon, next weekend.

'I'm happy to say that we, his family, will honour Dad's vision of this imaginative new event and his desire to bring honour, glory, recognition and financial help to those who need it most. As sponsors, we will still provide all the prize money which, as you know, is designed to help our youngsters. Opportunities can be lean for those trying to take their first steps into the adult world and Dad has always done his best over the years to help where he can. I will ensure that our family continues his legacy of benevolence for as long as we are able.'

The pub exploded with cheers and claps and 'Good old Rik!', 'Well done, Vic!' and other heartfelt calls. The speech wrapped up, the wake continued and the bar got ever busier.

Like a slowly meandering python, Pete the Prowl, beer in hand, slithered through the tight clusters of people, smiling sympathetically, an odd word here and there, his free hand gently touching the occasional shoulder, his eyes flitting constantly around the room. Hair slicked back, his dark suit noticeably shiny, his respectful appearance blemished only by a gaudy pocket handkerchief, he was watched by the three men at the bar.

'He never gives up,' said Bill quietly. 'I reckon it's become instinctive for him now, like an old lion always on the lookout in an aging pride. How old is he now, mid-fifties? I wonder how much success he has.'

'Not as much as you might imagine,' Bob chuckled. 'But he always lives in hope. Never been married but it's not for want of trying. I think Eve's resigned to the fact that she'll never be a grandmother.'

Across the room, they saw Eve, ample and distinctive in a colourful dress, chatting enthusiastically to her usual group of elderly friends. Catching her eye, Bob raised a glass in her direction, reciprocated by a smile and raised sherry.

A bustle and an 'Excuse me!' or two through the crowd, and the lanky figure of Colin, his wild snow-white hair bouncing, joined them at the bar. Well known in the village for his infectious enthusiasm for anything historical and cultural and especially his favourite hobby, photography, it was somewhat surprising not to see his usual accoutrement of a camera slung around his neck. Instead, a tatty tartan tie drooped sloppily from his neck to complete the image of the dishevelled academic. Smiling broadly despite the occasion, he shuffled in next to Bob.

'Another one, chaps?' he asked in his excitable voice. More beers ordered and pleasantries exchanged, Colin leant in conspiratorially close to his friends, hunched forward and eyes wide.

'You'll never guess who I bumped into this morning,' he began. 'Do you remember, well maybe you don't, that South African chap who came to the museum last year, an expert on Samuel Taylor Coleridge? I told you about him at the time.'

The others looked blank.

'Anyway', continued Colin, 'I just bumped into him again. Last year, he asked me whether there was anything in the museum archive about Coleridge that might help his studies, as Coleridge liked this area, Kubla Khan and all that. I looked but couldn't find anything new. Well, he's back in the village now, on holiday apparently, and he recognised me and asked if I'd found out anything else in the meantime. I told him that I hadn't – well, in truth, I haven't looked again but I'm sure there's nothing else in the museum that we don't already know. But…he did seem remarkably persistent.'

'Oh, yes?' said Vince, his interest piqued.

'Well, yes. I mean, he seems like a lovely bloke, a true academic, interested in all things historical, antiquities and stuff, even asked about local shipwrecks but, I don't know, there was something…overly pushy in the way he was asking me questions, quite direct at times. I'm sure it's just his manner but it started to get a bit unnerving.'

'Sounds a bit strange,' said Bob, 'but, then again, academics can be a strange lot.'

'Yes,' said Colin, considering, 'That must be it – just his manner. Nice bloke, though; name of Bram.'

'Did he ask about anything else?' asked Vince, his ex-copper's nose twitching.

'No, not really. He was just very inquisitive about everything. I just felt that his questioning, and there was a lot of it, was a bit too…intense.'

'Well,' said Vince, 'I'm sure he's okay but, just in case, be wary of him. Your instincts are usually pretty good, Colin.'

The groups of people were breaking up and reforming, the volume of chatter and laughter increasing as empties piled up on every surface. Ties were loosened, tales were exchanged, banter and good cheer. Bill peeled off from the bar, encouraged by a wave from across the room, Colin sloped off somewhere, and Vince and Bob decided to join Eve who'd moved away from her friends and had been joined by her son Pete.

'Mum was just telling me about Rik,' Pete told them when they arrived. 'They were good friends, especially when they were younger, before Rik joined the Navy.'

'He was a lovely man,' said Eve, her sad eyes lowered, 'and very handsome. I've never told you, Peter, but we were sweethearts for a short while, well before you were born. Nothing came of it, of course. He just wanted a more exciting life than this place could offer back then and he just went. When he returned, we stayed friends. Such an awful way to go but at least he found his excitement.'

'We became friends after he returned from the sea,' mused Bob, 'although he was much older than me. He treated everybody the same, generously, whatever their age or background. He'll be remembered for a long time and his legacy will last, especially if the triathlon is successful and becomes an annual event.'

As Vince and Bob consoled Eve, Pete's eyes continued to scan the room before, 'Ah, I've just spotted an old friend, haven't seen her for ages!' And, without another word, he quickly threaded his way towards a group of young women, smoothing back his hair as he went.

The others watched him go.

'That boy,' murmured Eve, rolling her eyes.

2

The following evening, the late September sun warmed the hamlet of Porlock Weir, the ancient small port linked to Porlock village close by. Promenaders lazily strolled along the quiet harbour watching the slowly rising tide. Children perched on the walls, buckets and crab lines dangling, the occasional squeal of capture as parents watched on vigilantly.

The weather-beaten benches outside the Bottom Ship pub were all full. Families, couples, walkers, locals, dogs, all enjoying the early evening glow with drinks, snacks and enticing dishes on the tables. All was peaceful, the boats swaying gently in the harbour as the tide rose ever higher and, far out in the bay, a few yachts slid sublimely through the shimmering waves.

Inside the pub, relaxing after another long day in the fields, were Raymond, Jack and Spider, seasoned farmers all, on stools at the end of the bar, tired but cheery. Jack, 31, had driven them all down as usual from their farms on the moor, his battered and bruised Land Rover parked outside, to be driven back later by whoever had had the least to drink, which was normally Raymond, the eldest of the bunch at 66. Spider, Jack's manager on his second farm and slightly younger than his boss, ordered the second round. Close to them were the youngsters, raucously into their third game of darts, the windowsill crowded by a row of full shot glasses next to several empty ones, and surrounded by pints.

'Gotcha!' shouted Dan as his dart hit the board. 'You're out, Ron, and another shot for me!'

As Dan downed one more, the men at the bar contentedly watched the game from a distance.

'It's great to see Dan and Anne letting their hair down,' observed Jack, 'after everything that's happened recently and their grandad's funeral yesterday.'

'They're coping with it well,' agreed Spider. 'They're a close family and so they'll be okay. The rumours about Rik's death will soon die down.'

More shouts and laughter from across the room as the darts zipped and thudded, all taking turns to try to knock out the others as Ron sat to one side, cheering them on. Mark, tall and solid, threw next and his darts all landed well.

'He's a good lad, that Mark,' said Raymond. 'A great worker, strong as an ox, never grumbles, and a very promising carpenter. He's just finished fixing my barn door.'

'He did a couple of my gates last week as well,' replied Jack. 'I agree, a great chippie and good all-round help. He uses my workshop sometimes, wants to get into craft woodworking more and I'm happy to teach him when I can. He's coming on well.'

'The last time I was there,' said Spider, 'the workshop was full of panto costumes.'

'Well, yes,' replied Jack with a smile. 'Laura was using the workshop to do some repairs to the costumes but she's done that now so they've all gone back.'

'What's the panto this year, then?' asked Raymond.

'Peter Pan,' Jack replied with a wry smile and a twinkle in his eye. 'I'm playing Smee, Captain Hook's chubby bosun. I wanted to do the panto again this year and that's about the only character that suits me, apparently.'

'I'd have thought you'd make a lovely Tinker Bell,' smirked Spider. 'Or even Captain Hook himself.'

'Mark would make a good Captain Hook,' observed Raymond. 'I mean, he's got the, what do you call it…the bearing, the height, the presence.'

'I don't think he's interested in going on the stage,' replied Jack. 'He's got other worries at the moment, financial. I wish I could give him more work, but things are tight right now, as you know.'

'Yes', said Raymond. 'I've been working the farm all my life and it's getting tougher. The price of everything seems to be increasing. It's not easy but we just get on with it, lads, don't we? At least we make a decent living, not like most of the youngsters around here.'

'Rik had the right idea,' said Jack. 'This triathlon – pure genius! It'll help those who need it most and bring much-needed income to the area. Every B&B and hotel's fully booked, I've heard.'

Another mighty yell from across the room, lots of laughter, tourist heads turning, and a couple of choice expletives from Mark who turned away from the board with a smile as Anne downed another shot. Grabbing his pint, Mark sauntered over to the men at the bar.

'Been knocked out,' he told them with a wobbly smile as he approached. 'I'm usually good at Killer but I think the shots have done for me. Mind if I join you?'

He pulled up a stool and settled his heavy frame upon it, his beer glass threatening to spill its contents before he placed it determinedly on the bar.

'We were just talking about the triathlon next week,' Raymond told Mark. 'I hear you've entered.'

'That's right,' replied Mark. 'I don't know how well I'll do but, to be honest, I'll try my best as I need the cash. They're putting my rent up next week and things are tight for Beth and me, 'specially as Amy's growing so fast. I know you guys give me as much work as you can, and I am really, really, really thankful to you all for that. But then again, most of my mates are in the same boat.'

Jack and Spider smiled at each other. Mark, normally quite considered and quiet, always became more chatty after a few drinks and, even after a few more, he always stayed happy and harmless.

'I mean,' Mark went on, staring into his beer, 'I love Porlock but we may have to move somewhere else, somewhere we can afford. It's all these second homes, holiday homes, putting prices up. None of us can afford these increasing rents and, as for buying somewhere, not a hope in hell. And that new development they're building - all posh homes, no affordable housing.'

'I agree, it's a scandal,' Jack said strongly. 'Nothing in the village for the next generation any more. The government won't do anything about it. Before too long, Porlock will turn into a holiday park in the summer and ghost town in the winter. Something has to be done.'

'If anything is done,' replied Mark, 'it'll probably be too late for me but I don't want to move from here.'

Raymond, recognising the signs of impending gloom in Mark who was normally so positive, rapidly changed tack.

'It sounds as if this triathlon will be a real help to you all,' he said. 'I don't really know what it's all about so why don't you tell me?'

'Ah,' said Mark, animated once more, 'it's going to be a laugh.' He took a slurp of beer.

'Go on,' encouraged Spider.

'Well, you know what a normal triathlon is – swimming, cycling, running? Rik had this idea to do an Exmoor version of it, with kayaking instead of swimming, horse riding instead of cycling and a bit of running as well, all around Porlock. It starts on the beach at Bossington where you kayak the mile or so to Porlock Weir; then get on your horse and ride through the woods to the rec in Porlock; then run down across the fields to finish at the Weir. And free drinks here at the pub for everyone who makes it.'

'Sounds far too tiring for me,' quipped Raymond.

'Ah, well, I don't like to say it, Raymond, but you're too old for it anyway. It's only open for those aged 18 to 30 as he wanted it to help us young 'uns. Oh, and only for those on, what did he say, 'limited means'. I think he means those who aren't earning much or who don't have money in the family. And locals only, who live in the area. I applied and was accepted, like some of my mates. Dan wanted to do it but, as he's Vic's grandson, wasn't allowed, you see. There's quite a few of us taking part.'

'I heard that the prize money is very generous,' said Jack. 'It should attract a lot of competitors.'

'I think it will,' said Mark, his words starting to slur a bit as his speech became more lively. '£2000 to the winner – can you believe it? – £1000 for second place, £500 for third and, guess what, £50 for everyone else who finishes! Rik was a very generous man, heart of gold. And Vic is like his dad, a lovely man.'

Final rowdy cheers and jeers from across the room. The last shots were sunk and darts stowed as the youngsters finished their last game and ambled merrily over to the others.

'And Anne and Dan here,' continued Mark, standing up and putting his arms around their shoulders as they arrived, 'are helping with the training up at the farm, for anyone who wants it.'

Anne smiled up at Mark. 'You don't need any training on my horses, big man. Everyone knows you're one of the best riders in the area.'

'Well, yes,' replied Mark. 'I think I can do well in the riding bit but I'm not so sure about the running and kayaking. But I've been running regularly for the last few weeks and been practicing in the kayak so I should do reasonably well.'

'You'll probably sink the kayak, the size you are!' laughed Dan.

More pints were ordered and the light-hearted banter continued. The few weeks since Rik's death had been difficult for them all, in their own ways. Dan and Anne, the elder grandchildren, seemed to be coping well, both immersed in helping their father Vic in readjusting the estate to the new order, Dan now second-in-command and Anne still up to her eyes in her riding business. The family was wealthy but the wound was deep.

Raymond, Jack and Spider enjoyed the company and the boisterous youthful frivolity of the evening. Encouraged by a couple more drinks and gently nudged by Mark and fellow farm hand Ron to remember the Exmoor farmer's tradition of helping local youngsters where they can, they all agreed to a small sweepstake for the triathlon – a modest prize to the winner but most of the money raised to be added to the winning pot.

The revelry continued inside as, outside, the light in the sky slowly faded. Fewer and fewer footsteps passed by and the crying of the gulls gradually ceased as the sun dipped serenely into the glowing sea.

****

The lights in Porlock Weir died, one by flickering one. A bright moon rose on the ink-black bay as the high tide fell and the old ropes creaked. A shadow flitted in the silvered light and there she stood, her gaze fixed to sea. A black shawl wrapped, her face set like stone, in silence, alone, her vigil not done.

A light breeze arose and, on top of the flagpole, the old cap rocked gently. She looked up, she smiled and stifled a tear. Then something brushed her soul and she felt the air shift. Something was coming, of that she was sure, in this wind full of whispers, like ghosts from the past.

The silence was cut by a long howl from the woods. A cloud passed the moon and then she was gone.

3

In a quiet rural corner of Porlock Vale, in a room darkened by drawn curtains despite the bright sunlight outside, on either side of an old wooden table, a large pot of strong tea between them, sat two people. They gazed at each other in silence, both faces beset with worry. One poured the tea, set down the pot and, with a deep sigh, began.

T: 'It may be just a coincidence. He may be what he says he is, just an academic. We may be worried for nothing.'

M: 'That's true, he may be. Coleridge experts love to visit the area, after all. He may be harmless. But, from what I've heard, he's asking too many other questions, about the coastline, local legends and shipwrecks. We must be on our guard. Especially now.'

T: 'I agree, we need to take it seriously. We're so close.'

M: 'The questions he's asking, he's just fishing. He can't know anything definite otherwise he'd come here with all guns blazing, so to speak.'

T: 'I'm sure you're right. He doesn't know who we are or what we do, and it's got to stay like that.'

M: 'It's possible that Fan's heard about him too. But we haven't been contacted yet.'

T: 'That's another thing I'm worried about. Fan's been silent for a while and I wondered if Rik was Fan. Rik's from a very old Exmoor family and has always been a very generous benefactor. And he had the connections for the gold.'

M: 'And there've been rumours that Rik's death wasn't natural? Because of all the suspicious deaths over the years, maybe the rumours started because of that?'

T: 'It's possible. If it's true, it means there's just the two of us now.'

M: 'So we have to be even more on our guard.'

T: 'But if we've been rumbled, I'm sure we'd know about it by now. I think the secret's still safe.'

M: 'Maybe. Maybe not. Which is why we're here.'

T: 'Yes.' A pause. 'Let's get back to the business in hand.'

They both took a sip of tea and looked in to each other's eyes.

M: 'This South African. He turns up now, asking questions. Those that have met him think he's shifty.'

T: 'Let's hope he's just an academic as he says. But, if he is on our trail, it proves we've made the right decision about the gold.'

M: 'We always knew that someone might find the Donna Maria story on the internet sooner or later.'

T: 'Thank God it's all gone now. 'One final grand gesture', Fan said in the note. In a way, I'm relieved it's almost over. It's been a heavy burden. But it's also a shame in a way.'

M: 'It is but we've done the right thing. It's all got to end now, before anybody finds out what's been going on.'

T: 'The South African - we'll have to keep a very close eye on him, just in case. And put the word around that he's up to no good and can't be trusted. Academic or not, we'll know soon enough.'

M: 'Only two more days to go, then it'll all be over.'

T: 'I hope so. I spoke to our contact yesterday and everything's on track. And I sent out the requests for help with the organisation of it all, anonymously of course, so let's hope everyone's on board. I can't wait to see the faces of everyone on Saturday. I'm hoping they'll all be – what's the word? – gobsmacked.'

M: 'How can they fail to be?'

The two finished their tea and then one went into the kitchen and returned with a chilled bottle of champagne and two glasses.

T: 'To celebrate the end of all of this and to toast the success of the new venture!'

M: 'I'll drink to that. By the way, did you bring your coin?'

The glasses were filled and then each took out one dulled gold coin, an ancient escudo, and laid it on the table.

M: 'The very last of the gold, one each for you and me and one for Fan. For posterity and as a souvenir, for the last ever guardians.'

They raised their glasses, smiling.

T: 'To the end of an era. And hopefully the start of a new one.'

4

The midday water lapped high in the sparkling harbour, the gentle waves slapping the bright sides of the bobbing boats and yachts tied tightly to their ropes. Ice-creamed families sauntered, eager dogs pulled, coffees were enjoyed at umbrellaed tables, the smells of seaweed and sun cream and chips. Another tranquil and endless lunchtime at Porlock Weir.

From the small garden behind the ancient thatched cottage that rested adjacent to the rocky beach came the sound of giggling. The open garden was flanked by straggly flower beds interspersed with large rocks while the patchy grassed area merged almost seamlessly into the grey sea-washed blanket of pebbles that spread out to form the ancient strand that sloped gently down to the quietly swishing water. A weather-beaten small slide, a more recent tricycle, a chewed football and a fading kayak were strewn across this semi-private space while, in the centre of what could be called the real garden, mother and child played.

Kat watched them from her kitchen window as she washed the crockery, and smiled. Beth was a loyal and loving daughter-in-law and mother to her only grandchild, Amy. It was such an idyllic scene on this peaceful afternoon and yet Kat's nerves were still strained, her sleep unsettled, worries besetting her every moment. Behind her, seated at the scarred oak table and chatting, were her son Mark and her friend Pete, invited for lunch.

Kat finished the washing and drying, laid the table, assembled the simple fare and called in the others. An enjoyable and unhurried lunch over which the hopes and dreams of Mark and his young family were shared; of Mark's ambition to become an artisan carpenter, of his general work on the farms across Exmoor, of his training for the upcoming triathlon, of his pride in his family.

As they chatted, Amy, golden blonde and scarcely two years old, bored of adult talk and leaving most of her sandwich in scraps on the table or the floor, slid off her chair and went to play with Noddy the dog who was resting, one eye open, in a shadowed corner. Noddy, a huge black dog believed to be a Croatian sheepdog crossed with a mastiff, was of formidable appearance although, to those who knew him, he was friendly, bright and a real softie, especially with Amy. She cuddled down with him and he contentedly lay still.

'Noddy's so good with her,' commented Pete, watching them.

'Has always been,' said Kat, 'since she was born. It's his Croatian blood – he knows his countrymen. He's so loving and gentle with his family but has this wild side. Like me,' she smiled.

'Does he still wander through the woods at night?' Pete asked. 'I think I hear him occasionally but I'm never too sure if it's him or the foxes.'

'Yes, he still goes out and howls at the moon some nights. He chases rabbits and sometimes gets one. But he still doesn't bother the pheasants or cause any trouble so the gamekeepers don't mind him and they all know him anyway. He never wanders far and always finds his way home before dawn.'

As if aware that he was the topic of conversation, Noddy raised his large head to look at Kat, causing Amy to stumble to her feet, grab a ball and run through the open door into the garden.

'Looks as if it's playtime again,' said Beth, standing. 'Come on, Mark, you can help me tire our young lady out before her nap.'

They followed Amy into the garden, accompanied by Noddy who never missed a chance to chase balls.

Inside, Kat took another couple of beers from the fridge and sat back down at the cluttered table opposite Pete. She looked him in the eye for a few silent seconds before lowering her gaze.

'What is it, Kat?' he asked, taking her hand, concern on his furrowed brow. 'I know you've gone through troubled times, with Croatia, Will, and everything else, but you're strong, always have been.'

'I know,' she replied, looking up at him. 'It's been difficult but…I'm here now, safe and as secure as I'll ever be, I suppose. Porlock has been good to me, lovely and welcoming. Especially you, Pete, you've been a good friend. I sometimes think you're the only one who knows me.'

'You don't let many people in, Kat,' Pete replied, gently squeezing her hand. 'We've known each other since you came back with Will, a long time now. And Will and I were friends from school here. I knew you were coming to a land you didn't know and with little Mark as well. Your English wasn't so good then but now, well, you're both now locals and not many here still remember what you went through.'

She smiled, a little sadly. 'That was long ago. Fate brought me to England, to Porlock. I was lucky to have met Will during the independence war.' She brightened. 'Did I tell you that we nearly shot each other when we first met? I was in a ruined building in Sisak, rifle in hand, ready to die for my people and then the British mercenaries stormed the building. When both groups came together, we both almost opened fire, until we recognised them for what they were and they saw that we were freedom fighters, just in time. We joined forces, Will and I got to know each other and, well, here I am now.'

'And with Mark as well. I know he knows how he came here but he's just one of us now, like you.'

'We couldn't leave him, Pete, you know that. We saw the baby, abandoned, his parents probably dead, and we couldn't leave him. Will and I were falling in love and so, when Will decided he'd had enough of the hell, we got out while we could, with Marco as he was known then.'

'Almost thirty years ago,' mused Pete, 'although it must seem a lifetime away for you.'

'It does,' replied Kat. 'Will tried hard to put all of that behind him, to go home and live a simple life, as a fisherman.' She wiped the beginnings of a tear from her eye. 'I still don't know what happened that day, the day he didn't come back. An accident? Rubbish! He was a good fisherman, his boat was good, the weather was good!'

'Now, calm down, Kat,' Pete said, sensing that she was about to flare up yet again. 'I know you think there was foul play somehow but there was no evidence of that, and no reason for it either. He was well-loved here, had lots of good friends. The verdict was accidental – his boat hit some rocks and must have sunk quickly, that's all. The tide was rising quickly and the currents here are vicious, you know that. That's why his body was never found.'

'I still think there's more to it,' she replied. 'He was sometimes very secretive, hiding something from me, like he knew something he shouldn't. You know we had worries about money, were struggling. Some mentioned suicide but Will was stronger than that and would never leave me and Mark, I'm sure of it. No, there was something else, my instincts tell me.'

'It must be your witch-blood,' Pete smiled. 'You once told me your family was from ancient Romanian stock, from a line of shamans or seers or something.'

He coaxed a smile back from her. 'It's true,' she admitted, 'though it sounds very fanciful nowadays. My mother had the gift of seeing, premonition, and I think I have the same gift. And my instinct tells me that something is not right about Will's death. Like Rik's death too, something odd. Too many 'accidental' deaths in these parts, it seems to me.'

'That was just a tragic accident as well,' said Pete. 'These things happen, Kat.'

'Maybe,' she replied pensively. 'But still I have doubts. I fly his cap from the flagpole and wait for him, in case. It's only been five years, after all. And if there is evil waiting to return here, I keep my rifle and hunting knife under my bed, and will use them if I need to.'

'I don't doubt you, Kat. You've still got that fire in your blood.'

Kat leant over and kissed Pete gently on the cheek. 'Thanks for understanding, and for listening. You've always been a good friend to me. I still don't know why you've never married.'

'It was that Spanish woman a long time ago,' Pete replied wistfully, 'the one I told you about. I was only young at the time, sailing around the Med as a carefree youngster. Her name was Sofia, the most beautiful woman I have ever seen. A long and wonderful summer. We fell in love, had a wild and passionate romance, and then we had to return to our other lives. I was heartbroken.'

'But that was long ago,' said Kat. 'You must have had other loves since?'

'Well, yes,' replied Pete. 'But none that have ever felt close to what I felt for Sofia. Everyone else seems to fall short and I don't want to settle for anything less. I think it's my distant Spanish blood that drew me to her.'

'So your dark Spanish eyes keep you on the prowl now, for love or just for fun?'

Pete smiled. 'I know they call me Pete the Prowl but I don't mind. I've given up trying to find love and instead just enjoy chatting up the ladies, for the fun of it – nothing serious ever. I know it looks superficial but it's my way of hiding stuff, the way we all have to sometimes. And I have lots of friends in the village too and enjoy company, so I'm never on my own. It's what I'm used to and I enjoy it. I'm too old to change now.'

'Never too old, Mister Prowler. Life is full of unexpected surprises.'

Outside, Mark, Beth, Amy and Noddy were having fun in the garden. Kat got up, looked through the window at her blossoming family, then returned to the table with a sigh.

'There's something else, Kat, isn't there?' asked Pete.

'Yes,' she replied. 'There is. I…I wanted to talk to you about Mark.'

'Go on,' prompted Pete.

She took a deep breath. 'I'm worried about him,' she started. 'You know he's really struggling to keep the money coming in. It's so difficult these days for young families, the rising cost of living. Well, Mark is a proud man and puts on a brave face but…he's in trouble.'

'What sort of trouble?' asked Pete, concerned.

'Money,' she said quietly. 'Don't tell anybody, but Mark and Beth are about to get evicted from their house. His rent will be increased soon and he's already behind two months. He doesn't know what to do.'

'Surely his landlord will be tolerant, give him a few more months to sort something out?'

'Mark's already asked,' Kat said, 'but the landlord refused. Said he needed the house to make more money. He wants to turn it into another flippin' holiday let, driving the locals out - yet again. If something can't be done, Mark will have to leave the village, move somewhere cheaper, away from here.'

'I had no idea it was that serious,' said Pete. 'They've nearly finished building that new cul-de-sac in the village but all of those are bound to be bought as more second homes or holiday lets, so they'll be no use to Mark or other youngsters. It's an impossible situation. I wish I could help but I don't have much myself, as you know.'

'Oh, Pete,' said Kat with a smile, 'I wasn't asking you, love. I know you'd do what you can. But I don't think much can be done. Mark works as hard as he can, the farmers give him as much work as they can, and he's hoping to win something in this triathlon, at least to keep the wolves from the door for a short while. No, Pete, I don't know if anything at all can be done. I'm just off-loading on you, sorry.'

'Don't be sorry, Kat.' Pete replied. 'I can always put the word around, see if anybody else has jobs for him.'

'Thanks, anything would help. I give him as much as I can from the cleaning and the cakes I make for Sam's bakery but it's not much. I was hoping to have my own cake shop here at the Weir by now, as you know, but it's more important to help Mark now. I don't want him to move away.'

Pete squeezed her hand reassuringly. 'I'll do what I can, love.'

A shadow in the room heralded the return of Mark followed by Beth, carrying a flagging Amy, and Noddy, who flumped back down in his favoured spot. Lunchtime over, hugs and kisses, and they all prepared to get back to their afternoon busyness – Mark to a quick job close by, Beth and Amy off home, and Pete back to his restoration workshop, possibly via the pub.

Outside, as the family drove off waving, Kat took Pete's hand.

'Thanks again, for listening.'

'Any time,' Pete replied. 'I'm always here for you, you know that. And try not to worry too much.'

'I'll try,' she smiled, 'but it's difficult sometimes. I have this strong feeling that something big is about to happen but I don't know if it's going to be good or bad.'

'You're just worried about Mark,' reassured Pete. 'We'll work something out, somehow.'

***

As Pete in contemplation walked towards his car, he noticed the figure of a tall swarthy man in khaki trousers, loose flowery shirt, Panama hat and shades standing and staring at the row of thatched cottages. A camera slung over one shoulder completed the image of the curious tourist and yet his static pose suggested study more than just idle curiosity. As Pete was about to pass him, the man turned quickly, a sudden broad smile lighting up his tanned and stubbled face.

'Ah!' he barked, stopping Pete in his tracks. 'Sorry to bother you. Do you live here?'

South African, fifties.

'Yes,' said Pete warily. 'Up in the village. How can I help you?'

'I was just wondering about the history of these cottages,' the man replied. 'I love British history and visit whenever I can. I'm doing a bit of research in the area and these cottages look very old. Must have been here when Porlock Weir was a busy

24

fishing port. Might have even been involved in the smuggling that went on in these parts. I understand that all sorts of contraband came through this area. Alcohol, clothes, tobacco. Gold.'

'Quite possibly,' said Pete nonchalantly. 'Lots of these places had secret compartments, false walls, that were used to hide smuggled goods. So they say.'

'Fascinating. The things that must have gone on here, the secrets that were kept,' the man mused, watching Pete intently. 'I'm Bram, by the way, Bram de Jong. Researcher, collector, just on holiday here. From South Africa.'

Pete shook the proffered hand. 'I'm Pete,' he replied. 'Furniture restorer and beer lover. Somerset born and bred. So, a researcher and collector?'

'That's right,' replied Bram genially. 'I study Samuel Taylor Coleridge, the poet, and I like to collect antiques and antiquities. While I'm here on holiday, I thought I'd try to find out more about Coleridge and pick up some antiques while in the area. Coleridge wrote Kubla Khan near here so must have visited Porlock Weir on several occasions. When all that smuggling was still going on.'

'I suppose so,' mumbled Pete.

'As you've lived here all your life,' the man continued, 'you must know all the local legends. Have you heard anything about a famous shipwreck here, a few hundred years ago? Maybe a Spanish ship?'

'You mean, from the Armada times?' asked Pete, interested.

'Yes,' Bram replied, 'or maybe later.'

'I don't think so. I mean, there've been plenty of wrecks along this coast for centuries but I've never heard about a Spanish one. What would a Spanish ship be doing in these waters?'

'Oh, I don't know. Maybe it came when we weren't at war with them, or it was captured in battle. They were turbulent times when fortunes could be made.'

Bram was peering intently at Pete as if expecting some revelation. Pete caught his eye as Bram quickly turned his gaze away.

'No,' said Pete firmly. 'Never heard of anything like that. Why do you ask?'

'Oh, it's nothing really,' Bram said dismissively. 'Just another legend that sounded interesting. As I said, I like that sort of thing – history, antiquities.'

Pete kept his eyes fixed on the man who was looking at the cottages again. Then he had a thought.

'I was just wondering, Bram – are you staying in the area?'

'Yes, in a B&B in the village. I'm here for a couple of weeks. Why do you ask?'

'Well,' Pete went on. 'My mother is clearing out some old things, she's convinced she's going to die soon, and she has lots of old jewellery, most of it probably worthless. If you're good at identifying antiques, would you mind having a quick look at the stuff, to see if there's anything valuable there? I'd be very grateful and there'll be a couple of pints in it for you.'

Bram's face lit up. 'I'd be happy to. I'm here for the old stuff. Let me know where and when.'

The men parted amiably after arranging to meet in The Top Ship the following night, Friday. As Pete reached his car, he turned to see that Bram had returned to the old cottages and was peering closely at them, almost scanning them, as he was when they first met.

Something seemed odd to Pete – the man was genial yet guarded and asked unusual and probing questions. And his eyes seemed to flash behind the shades that he never took off.

5

'I bet that's him,' said Bill.

Vince and Joe followed his gaze to see a tall, rugged, well-dressed man on his own being shown to a table in the adjacent bar by teenage Hannah, the newest member of staff. In perfect synchronisation, the three men lifted their pints to their lips, eyes fixed on the stranger, watching every move as he settled. He seemed at ease, glancing around the room before ordering a drink and then picking up the menu.

'Seems all right,' noted Vince, 'just a regular tourist.'

'Yup,' agreed Joe, the local butcher, who'd heard about Colin's misgivings. 'Not from these parts, though.'

The men, seated in their usual place by the bar and unlit fire, one coat covering a stool in case a friend dropped by, watched Hannah scurry to the bar for the drink. As she waited for it to be poured, Vince nudged her softly.

'Hey, love,' he asked. 'That man you've just seated. Does he have a foreign accent by any chance?'

'Oh yes,' she replied eagerly. 'Something foreign. I couldn't understand him at first. Australian, or Irish, French maybe, German? Funny accent.'

'Could it be South African?' Vince suggested.

'Could be,' replied Hannah vaguely. 'I'm not very good at languages. Could be Martian for all I know.'

The men chuckled and returned to their ales and crisps, ever watchful.

The evening was young and yet the pub seemed to fill up more quickly than usual, the entrance door almost constantly open as couples, groups, friends lined up to be seated or to be shown to the terraced garden under the late September sun. Most were visitors but all had an air of eager excitement, loud and boisterous chatter, more exuberant than a usual Friday night, that the three men in the corner didn't miss. Everyone was in a cheery mood, even the landlord, generally grumpy when the rush began but tonight enjoying the buzz and no doubt counting the cash. 'All these people,' murmured Bill. 'Must be here for this special event at the Weir tomorrow. I still don't know…'

'Hey,' interrupted Joe, 'there's Pete the Prowl just come in. He's heading for that bloke.'

They all watched Pete bustle his way through the small crowd towards the solitary man, greet him politely and then sit down opposite, placing a small wooden box on the table between them. Curious, they continued to watch from a distance.

After Hannah had delivered his drink, including the correctly-guessed pint for Pete, Pete opened the box and carefully placed the contents, one item at a time, onto the old wooden table. Chains of silver and gold, brooches of every colour, earrings, rings, an old coin or two, a delicate pearl necklace, a jewelled tie pin, and other bewitching miscellanea that sparkled and glinted in the soft glow of the table's candle. Bram's steely blue eyes lit up as he scanned the enticing array.

'I was about to order my meal,' he said to Pete, eyes fixed on the jewellery, 'but I think I'll wait. This collection looks interesting.'

Putting on a pair of glasses, Bram studied each item in turn, muttering brief comments for Pete's benefit. He put aside a couple of objects after scrutinizing them with more interest. Pete watched him with anticipation until, after many minutes and the best part of a pint, Bram sat back, took off his glasses and faced Pete, a smile on his face.

'I'm sorry to say that most of this is just costume jewellery, Pete,' he started. 'Mainly early 20th century, some Victorian, worth a little to collectors but nothing of real value.'

He saw the look of disappointment on Pete's face.

'But,' Bram continued, 'these two pieces that I've put aside, they are much more interesting. This,' he said, picking up the tie pin, 'and this,' picking up a thick and scratched gold ring set with a tarnished red stone.

'The tie pin,' he said, setting the items back down on the table, 'is, I think, mid-Victorian and seems to have three small diamonds in it, in very good condition. I'm no expert but it's worth getting it valued professionally. Could be worth a few hundred pounds.' Pete's eyes lit up.

Bram picked up the gold ring. 'Now this,' he said, staring intently at it as he turned it over in his fingers, 'is older. Where did it come from?'

Pete watched him studying the item, becoming as intrigued as Bram seemed to be.

'My mother's always had it. She once told me that she was given it as a token of love by one of her boyfriends here on the moor when she was young, before she met my father.'

Bram continued to turn the ring over and over in silence before setting it down on the table again. Both men finished their drinks and, as Hannah was passing, they ordered more.

'That makes sense,' Bram said eventually, slowly and deliberately. 'I've only seen two of these before and both were classed as love amulets. And very old – mediaeval.'

Pete stared at him. 'That's…how old?' he asked pensively.

'If this is what I think it is – and I'm fairly certain – this could be almost 500 years old. 16th century, possibly a bit later.'

Pete picked up the ring in disbelief, then looked at Bram. 'From Exmoor…I mean, British?'

'No,' replied Bram, 'from South America. This is, I believe, an Inca love amulet. The gold ring has a ruby setting. The ruby has two intertwined hearts carved into it and then, when the ruby is dipped into the blood of two lovers, it binds their blood and hearts together for all eternity, and their families. If you look closely you may be able to make out the shape of hearts cut into the stone.'

Pete peered hard and, sure enough, very faint scratches in the worn red stone could, with imagination, suggest hearts.

'In the 16th century,' Bram went on, 'the Spanish conquistadors fought the Incas and raided their treasures, bringing much of it back to Spain. This may be where this ring came from originally.'

Pete had some more beer, gathering his thoughts, still trying to understand what this all meant.

'And yesterday', Pete continued after the brief pause, putting his pint down, 'you mentioned a Spanish ship that might have come here a long time ago. If that legend's true, this ring may have come from there?'

'Well, it is possible,' said Bram, 'if the legend is true. But if it was, I would expect everyone here to know about it. Especially those whose families go back generations. Like you.'

'No,' replied Pete cautiously, avoiding Bram's gaze, 'I don't know anything like that, as I said. This ring could have come from anywhere.'

'You're right,' Bram said lightly, suddenly leaning back casually in his chair. 'A souvenir from travels, an antique shop, a gift. Probably nothing to do with legendary spoils of war.'

Pete, taking a measured sip from his pint that had just arrived, watched Bram carefully as the South African picked up the ring again, purposely studying it and avoiding Pete's eyes. A certain unease passed through Pete.

Breaking the silence at the table, Hannah appeared and Bram ordered from the menu. After a bit more small talk and a bit more beer, the awkward atmosphere slowly dissipated as Bram switched the conversation back to his favoured subjects, history and antiquities. And then, once geniality had been re-established, he slipped in a smiling proposal to buy Pete's ring. It was a generous offer that Pete, not knowing its true value and unwilling to part with an heirloom, politely refused. Upon which Bram, declining his head in gracious defeat, made his excuses and sauntered off to the men's room.

In the corner, Bill had left, replaced by Colin who'd popped in for an early evening drink. They'd all been watching discretely from across the room and now, with Bram away and their curiosity piqued, Vince decided to have a brief chat with Pete, joined by Colin who wanted to greet 'my South African chum,' leaving Joe to mind their table. Pete had put all the trinkets back in the box and, when the others arrived with questions, Pete quickly summarised their conversation. Further probing about Bram's character revealed Pete's misgivings: 'Seemed cagey, always on his guard but that might be just his manner'; 'Seems to know a lot about Porlock legends'; 'Talked a lot about antiquities'; 'Strangely, didn't mention Coleridge once.'

Colin, conscious that Bram could return at any moment, told Pete of his similar uncertainty. A quick decision to dig a bit deeper with Bram and, as Hannah was passing again, another quick decision by Vince to order more beers – 'Always helps to loosen the tongue.'

Almost on cue, Bram returned. Greetings over, Colin dived in enthusiastically to ask him about his interest in Coleridge, much to Bram's obvious discomfort at being unexpectedly mobbed. Bram stumbled through a tale of schoolboy interest in the Romantic poets that developed into a passion when he visited Exmoor for the first time many years ago and which encouraged him to become an academic researcher at Pretoria University.

The beers arrived, with the promise that Bram's meal would be ready soon. More lively and general Coleridge chat between Colin and Bram as the others spectated, Vince noting with hidden satisfaction that Bram's speech was becoming a bit more animated as the ale went down. A lull in the conversation and then a sudden thought appeared to come to Bram.

'Colin, my friend,' he beamed, his steely eyes glistening, 'I've been meaning to ask you something, about Coleridge here. Something about that Kubla Khan poem.'

'I know it,' Colin replied. 'Unfinished as Coleridge was famously interrupted by a visit from a man from Porlock'.

'That's the one,' said Bram. 'Well, you know in the poem there's that line 'Caves measureless to man, down to a sunless sea'?'

'I think it's 'caverns' in the poem, not 'caves',' replied Colin, frowning.

'Oh yes,' said Bram, 'my mistake, sorry. Anyway, I heard a rumour, can't remember from where, that the caves – caverns – in the poem might be based on real caves. Coleridge wrote the poem on the farm up on the hills close to the cliffs and might have seen a cave there that inspired him. I know it's just a rumour but do you know if there are any old caves over there, in the cliffs by the sea?'

Colin looked quizzically at Vince and Pete, who appeared both puzzled and bemused. When neither made any comment, Colin turned back to Bram.

'Well,' he said cautiously, 'I haven't heard anything like that. There may be a few old caves along the coastline but nothing big as far as I know. But I know someone we can ask. He does a lot of fishing, knows the coast like the back of his hand, says he's from an old smuggling family. If anyone knows, Bob will.'

'I'd be very grateful,' replied Bram. 'Anything to do with Coleridge. And I love the old legends from these parts too – smuggling, shipwrecks, ghosts, buried treasure, stories passed down by word of mouth, that sort of thing.'

'I did hear a local legend about one cave over there,' Vince mentioned. 'They say that the devil lives there and he'll drag people to a watery death if they disturb him.'

'I find,' said Bram slowly, 'that a lot of legends are based on a real story a long time ago. I've heard a lot of legends from all over the world and ignore most. But legends based on devils are truer than most, usually protecting something important with the threat of the ultimate evil. I'm a religious man and am, I admit, afraid of the devil. Well, the devil and wild dogs. Where I live, wild dogs are fearless and can tear anything apart within minutes. Scary to witness. They say that wild dogs are the souls of those cursed by witches.'

'You'd better keep away from those caves then,' said Vince gruffly. 'Stick to your books.'

'Good advice,' replied Bram with a slight slur. 'But, if your friend knows anything about any caves, I would still be interested. For my Coleridge research, of course.'

'Of course,' said Vince, glancing at the others. 'We'll let you know.'

Bram's meal arrived and so the others decided to leave him to it, bidding him farewell and returning to the bar.

'Well?' asked Joe as they settled back down.

'A suspicious character, in my mind,' Vince started, 'and I've known quite a few of them in my time.'

'He did seem to be hiding something,' observed Pete. 'Something a bit fishy about him. I thought the same when I met him yesterday.'

'He didn't even know the right words to Kubla Khan,' contributed Colin, usually one to see the best in people. 'Very odd for an expert.'

'Looks harmless to me,' said Joe. 'Just a regular tourist. They love all these local legends.'

'No, it's more than that,' insisted Pete. 'There's something else about him, I'm sure. The questions he's asking, he's probing for something. He's got an agenda, I don't trust him.'

'Exactly what I felt,' replied Vince, 'When I was in the force, I could spot a wrong 'un from a mile away. Call it copper's instinct.'

'There you go then,' replied Pete. 'We all think he's dodgy.'

'Looks okay to me,' said Joe quietly, taking a slurp.

'I made up that story about a local legend,' Vince continued, ignoring Joe. 'A devil

32

in a cave, to see how he'd react, as he seemed interested in caves, but he didn't really react. He may be what he says he is but, if not, we need to know what his agenda is. I don't trust him either. I agree with Pete - best to keep an eye on him.'

More chat, more banter, more beer and the men's humour quickly improved. The pub was in full swing, a constant stream to and from the bar, tables emptying and refilling, staff bustling, noisy, joyful, everyone in good cheer. The men's thoughts and discussion soon turned to the 'special event' tomorrow that had been the main topic of conversation in the village for days.

'I don't think anybody knows what's going to happen,' said Pete. 'Something big, everyone says, but we don't know anything else.'

'It's a mystery,' replied Vince. 'Someone's arranging something and word's got around to be at the Weir at midday tomorrow, but that's all we know.'

'I've been asked to provide sausages and burgers for a barbecue,' admitted Joe the butcher, 'and Sam's been asked to bring the rolls. But I don't know who's asked us – we just received envelopes with the requests, and the money to cover it.'

'We know that happens from time to time,' Pete said. 'Requests to help out with good causes and village events. I've been asked to help in the past and my costs were covered. My request, a few years back, just said it was from an anonymous benefactor.'

'The same for me this time,' replied Joe. 'It's always for the good of the community so nobody minds doing it.'

'Whatever it is, I'll bring my camera and take lots of photos,' said Colin enthusiastically. 'I'll definitely be there.'

'And me!'

'And me!'

'And me!'

6

Winding your way down the road to Porlock Weir, you would at first glance believe that it was a normal Saturday morning. Up in Porlock itself, the tourists were starting to stir, the traffic was slowly increasing, sight-seeing coaches, caravans, mobile homes, frustrated tractors, nervous horses, yapping dogs, young families dipping into shops. There was no indication than anything other than the usual was afoot, no posters, no signs, no whispers. But, to the locals and a few others in the know, there was an undercurrent of excited curiosity. Very gradually, the number of those walking the road down to the harbour started to grow.

Well before 11am, the car park was full as were the edges of the roads on the approaches. At the Weir, crowds were milling about, enjoying another warm and sunny day, watching the boats gently swaying in the light breeze as the tide filled the small harbour. The pub tables were fully occupied already, coffees and cakes, an early pint or three, bar staff bustling unusually early. On all the buildings facing the sea, colourful bunting had been put up during the night and, on the stony beach close by, a substantial barbecue and a hog roast were being set up next to a few trestle tables. Across the footbridge over the harbour water could be seen a couple of banks of large speakers flanking what appeared to be a small raised podium and lectern, cordoned off by ropes that were adorned with more bunting. Nothing else – no entertainers, no music, no stalls, no posters, no fanfare. All low-key.

As the time slowly crept towards midday, the enticing smells of cooking meat came from the beach where Joe the butcher was helping with the barbecue and hog roast alongside Sam the baker with his bread rolls. Kat was there preparing too, laying out her contribution of flamboyant cakes. They were all approached occasionally with questions about what was happening, when and why, but they all pleaded ignorance, admitting only that they'd been asked to help with this 'special event' and knew nothing more. A few members of the local press, all asked to attend at short notice, tried to push them further until they realised that everyone present was as in the dark as they were. Hungry enquiries were directed to the A-frame and its message – 'Not open until 1pm, approx.'

It seemed as if the whole of north Exmoor were there, families, individuals, couples from the villages, the vale and the moor. Rumours abounded but nobody could offer any firm details of what was in store. The road and harbourside filled up, people sitting on walls, on the grass and beach, some in deckchairs, all loitering, all waiting in an atmosphere of light-hearted festivity. A few high-vissed marshals joined the crowds, once again requested by person or persons unknown. Watches were checked regularly as the advertised time approached and, as midday came, everyone looked around expectantly, at the roads, the woods, the sea, the beach, the sky. Nothing.

And then a whistle blew, from the raised beach on the far side of the harbour. Heads turned towards the sound to see a figure on the edge of the beach waving wildly with two hands towards the massed crowd and appearing to shout something, although the words were indistinct. The figure, a man, continued to wave for a short while before disappearing from sight behind the row of cottages there. Everyone around the harbour looked perplexed. A few started to walk towards the beach and, when they reached it they could be seen to stop and stare out to sea. Others, in small groups at first but soon followed by the majority of the crowd, swarmed in the same direction. What they saw when they reached the beach stopped them all in their tracks.

Approaching distantly from the west and bound in their direction was a galleon in full mast. Its honey wood bright and its fittings shining in the sunlight, its sails were full in the breeze, bringing the mighty ship steadily towards Porlock Weir scarcely half a mile away and moving quickly. A frenzy of activity could be seen on board, crew scurrying about, on ropes, watching the sides, arms waving, orders no doubt being shouted. On the upper deck at the front, two figures stood, possibly a woman and a tall man wearing a hat, watching the approach. The crowd on land stared in awe.

A quarter of a mile away now, the sails on the three masts started to be taken in, the crew heaving, winding, tying, all hands on deck. The ship was close enough now for the crowds to see that the crew was dressed in some sort of period costume and could hear that the barked orders across the waves were not in English. As the ship started to slow, it gradually turned to head towards the harbour before, a couple of hundred yards from shore, it came to a gentle stop, rocking in the light swell. The anchors were dropped, bodies scurried around the deck, some seeming to take up positions at the sides where a row of cannons jutted out. The two at the front could be seen talking and watching the shore.

On land, everyone stared in wonder, puzzlement and some consternation. Uncertain mutterings of pirates, a film set, publicity stunt, foreign invasion and other fanciful guesses spread across the beach and into the hamlet, everyone taking photographs, the press eager for the story, pints left undrunk on the pub tables as all massed on every viewpoint available. All eyes were on the impressive ship on which the crew appeared to have stopped moving. A portly man in the centre of the deck could be seen raising one arm, holding it there for several seconds before lowering it swiftly. Instantaneously, a colossal BOOM! came from the ship followed immediately by plumes of smoke spouting from the four cannons that faced land. Even though the cannons were aimed to one side of the harbour, many on shore shrieked and instinctively ducked. Some tentatively cheered but most were a little unsure until, after the smoke had cleared, they saw all crew members on the ship line up on the deck facing the harbour, salute in unison and then wave happily to the crowds. Relief surged through the spectators who, now smiling happily once again, cheered and waved back.

On board, the figures all started moving to the stern of the ship where, a couple of minutes later, a red and yellow striped rowing boat containing five people could be seen gently set down in the sea and its cables released. The small wooden boat, powered by two oarsmen and carrying three passengers, swung professionally around and slowly started making its way towards the harbour. The tide was at its fullest when the boat approached the small jetty which had been cordoned off, as had been the land adjacent where the podium and speakers had been set up. Everyone watched with interest, speculating who these bizarre visitors - four men, one woman, with Mediterranean complexions and now clearly dressed as period seafarers - could be. The boat reached the jetty, was tied up by the oarsmen who then assisted the others out. The first up the steps was an elegant lady in a bright red ruffle dress, a flowered headband adorning long black hair, followed by a tall handsome man with a colourful wide-brimmed hat and grey long buttoned coat, and lastly an unshaven, slightly rotund man in loose trousers and flannel shirt. The oarsmen checked their knots and followed the others onto land.

Stopping briefly to survey the many hundreds of people who stood in murmuring anticipation all around, the exotic troupe made its way towards the podium and lectern, slightly elevated and fronted by a microphone on a stand. The tall man, appearing tentative, stepped up, took a folded sheet of paper and a small flag from his coat and placed them on the lectern, as the others in the party took up positions on either side. A sudden buzz from the speakers as the microphone was turned on and then, when the sound faded, the huge crowd fell silent, all waiting. The man on the podium, upright and face set with confidence, faced his audience.

He spread out his arms slowly, smiled and cried out, 'Hello, people of Porlock!'

Quite a few, bemused and intrigued, returned his greeting. The man bowed graciously in acknowledgment.

I hope that you can all hear me well?' A strong accent. 'I hope you weren't scared by our welcome salute? There were no balls in the cannons, believe me!'

Smiles in the crowd as the people started to settle, enjoying the spectacle and wondering what was to come.

'Let me introduce myself and my friends. My name is Ramon Ortega. This is my sister Elisa, this is my captain Sebastian and these two are some of the crew, Carlos and Fabio. We are all from Spain.'

Greetings called back from various parts of the throng as the other members of Ramon's group smiled and waved back.

'Now,' continued Ramon, glancing down at the lectern and looking more serious, as the calls from the crowd died down. 'You are wondering why we are here. What is this magnificent ship that you see out there? Why are we dressed so strangely? What do we want? Who are we? Well, my friends, I will tell you.'

He picked up the sheet of paper and held it aloft.

'I will read this out to you', he said. 'I think it will explain everything.'

He cleared his throat, unfolded the sheet and, slowly and clearly, began.

'Welcome to the people of Porlock, Porlock Weir and Porlock Vale. The ship that you see before you is a replica of a Spanish galleon of the 17th century, two-thirds of the actual size. It was built in Spain, in the shipyard that I and my family own.

'We have sailed from Spain to Porlock to arrive here today,' he continued. 'The ship has been built in honour of my great-grandparents, John and Maria. When Maria was young, she came to Porlock and fell in love with the place. She also fell in love with John, a young man who lived here and they went back to Spain and were married. They had a successful business in ship-building and, never forgetting Porlock, it was their desire and dream to help the village and so promised to give them a ship to make money by trading across the sea, a big business at the time. Porlock then was not a wealthy place and had no ships of its own. But, because of the Great War, the ship was sadly never built.

'However, due to fate and good fortune, we are now in a position to do what my great-grandparents unfortunately could not. We feel it is our family duty to honour the promise and dream of our ancestors by providing a ship – the one you see out there. From this moment onwards, that ship is given, entirely free of charge and obligation, by us to the people of Porlock, to be kept here and used to promote Porlock and Exmoor globally, to help secure the long-term prosperity of the area.'

A ripple of incredulity passed through the crowd, a few whoops and cheers but, in the main, most remained quiet, not willing to believe what they had heard and awaiting more elaboration.

'It has been agreed with the authorities that the ship's permanent mooring will be in the bay, free in perpetuity. It is not a trading ship, as those days have passed, but one to be used in another way. To ensure the ship and its crew are supported financially, the ship will be offering working holiday experience and ship-handling courses to anybody and, for approximately half of every year, it will travel the world to do the same.'

Some enthusiastic cheering from the audience as the astounding information started to sink in.

'Just one more thing,' said Ramon. 'I am almost finished, you will be happy to know. This is the last line.'

He picked up the flag that was lying on the lectern and peered at the speech again. 'The name of the ship is…the Porlock Maria!'

Upon which he turned towards the sea, lifted the flag high and waved it vigorously. Everyone looked towards the ship where, on the bow, a camouflaged sheet seemed to fall away revealing the name Porlock Maria. At the same time, a fluttering flag was hoisted on the main mast – the Exmoor flag.

The reality of this surreal event was finally brought home to the masses. Clapping, cheering, calls of support and friendship that continued for many moments. The Spaniards acknowledged the warm enthusiasm but remained where they stood, waiting for the hubbub to die down. When it did, Ramon faced the microphone one last time.

'The prepared speech is over but I would like to say more. This news is a big surprise to you all but what I have said is the truth, believe me. I am happy to answer any questions you have. There are two more things I would like to say.

'Firstly, my crew and I will be staying in Porlock for two weeks before returning home. In this time, we will recruit and train a new crew to run the ship when we are gone. From tomorrow, we will be asking for applications from anybody in Porlock Vale who may be interested.

'Secondly, it has been arranged that everyone here can have not only something from the barbecue, for free, but also a free drink from the pub!

'And lastly, before you all rush off, I and my crew would like to say thank you to everybody for welcoming us and we are looking forward to getting to know you all!'

Ramon stood down from the podium as the cheering crowd either started to move keenly towards the pub and the barbecue area or towards the Spaniards, to greet them properly and, no doubt, ask further questions.

At the back and watching with great interest were Jack and Raymond with George and John, all farm owners on the moor and all holding pints. Rarely surprised by the strange vagaries of mankind that they'd all witnessed over the years, they didn't join in with the cheering and clapping but instead stood quietly with puzzled frowns on their faces.

'Well, I wasn't expecting that,' began John.

'Nor me,' replied George, the oldest of the group. 'I think it's caught us all by surprise.'

'Must have cost a fortune,' considered Raymond. 'This Spaniard must be loaded. First Rik with his sponsoring the triathlon next weekend and now this. A lot of donations coming into Porlock at the moment.'

'Just a coincidence,' joined in Jack thoughtfully.

'If it's as he says,' said George slowly, 'the Spaniard has done a good thing. If it delivers what he says, it'll change Porlock forever and hopefully for the better. People round here need a boost, hope for the future, especially the young 'uns.'

'You're right, George,' said Jack. 'This place needs something to move it forwards, some plan to make sure the next generation stays. The government aren't doing anything for us so we have to think of something ourselves. Things might be starting to look up.'

'Hope so,' replied John. 'I'm interested to see how it develops. And, in truth, I'm getting tired of farming. Think I'll apply for a job on the ship, if I'm not too old. I fancy sailing off into the sunset.'

'Far too old, John,' chuckled Raymond. 'Stick to what you know, old timer. Now, let's go and have another drink, courtesy of our new Spanish friends. It's going to be an interesting couple of weeks.'

As they wandered off towards the pub, they passed close to a tall but unremarkable man in a Panama hat standing on his own.

'Much too coincidental,' Bram pondered to himself, smiling thinly.

He watched the crowds carefully and failed to notice that others were watching him carefully too.

***

That night, as the bright moon glistened over the quiet hamlet, as the lights in the houses were gradually extinguished, as the owls in the wood hooted in the eerie stillness, Kat stood and looked out to sea, still waiting, still hoping. The tide had fallen, the ship had moved further out, only a couple of lights still twinkling in its cabins. A peaceful end to an eventful day.

As she scanned the serene monochrome bay, her eye was caught by a disturbance in the water beyond the island. Something was moving there, a small rowing boat with one person aboard, too far away to identify, silently moving in the direction of the ship.

She smiled to herself. 'Something definitely in the air.'

In the deep shadows of the harbour, a tall man was watching too.

7

The following morning, out in a remote part of the vale, around the same wooden table and with a large pot of tea between them, the two sat and faced each other once again. They both smiled.

T: 'Well, that went smoothly, better than expected.'

M: 'Yes, Ramon did a great job, stuck to the script. I had a word with him last night and he's happy.'

T: 'A few necessary white lies but we've covered that. Someone's bound to check the story but there are no detailed records of his great-grandparents except that they started a successful ship-building company. And plenty of Johns emigrated from this part of the world at that time too.'

M: 'And Ramon's sorted out the paperwork his end to show that the ship was fully financed by himself. His accountants are happy – put it down as a charitable donation.'

T: 'Good. So he's fully paid now. You gave him the gold?'

M: 'I did. You should have seen his eyes when he opened the chest. He could hardly believe that the last of it's being returned to Spain after all these centuries. He's arranged to move it back tomorrow. And he told me how proud he was to help us out at the same time.'

T: 'Does he know the full story?'

M: 'Most of it, not all. About the history, the wrecking, the guardians. He doesn't know about Fan, just thinks it's the two of us doing all this.'

T: 'And he knows that we're ghosts, that we have to stay invisible to everyone?'

M: 'Yes, he knows that.'

T: 'Do you trust him?'

M: 'I do. He's very smart. He knows that we've always done it for the community and he understands the secrecy. If any of this comes to light, heads will roll, his and ours. He knows that.'

T: 'I must admit, I'm glad it went well. All the paperwork has been done, the authorities are happy, the people seem happy. Our job is almost over. But…we might have another problem.'

M: 'Oh yes?'

T reached into a pocket, withdrew a sheet of paper, unfolded it and put it onto the table for M to read. Typed, short and to the point, it read, 'The South African has been identified as a threat. Highly likely that he knows the secret. He must go. Send ideas by return,' with the drop-off point added.

M: 'From Fan?'

T: 'Yup. At least we know now that Rik wasn't Fan. It came through my letterbox overnight. We thought the South African was suspicious and Fan agrees with us. Looks like we have more work to do.'

M: 'If the South African does know what's been going on, he's too late anyway. I mean, if he's just a treasure-hunter, all the gold has now gone. If he's a private investigator, our tracks are covered. If he's still sniffing around, it means he doesn't know the full story yet. And that's assuming he is who we think he is and not just an innocent but nosy academic as he claims.'

T: 'You're right, he may be innocent. We're not sure and, from the note, Fan's not a hundred per cent sure either. We need to scare him off which shouldn't be too difficult if he's clean. We have to avoid the ultimate deterrent, far too dangerous nowadays, but we must do whatever's necessary to keep the secret safe, as always. Having everything exposed now is not an option.'

So saying, more tea was poured and the two got down to business. As is not uncommon in small communities, tongues wag and word had spread around the village about Bram, his Coleridge research and his interest in caves along the coast. The two decided to use this angle as a lure.

After an hour or so, they had a plan.

8

'Welcome aboard!'

Ramon stood on deck, greeting his guests cheerfully as they arrived. A gloriously sunny Sunday morning when the Porlock Maria was open to anybody who'd like to visit, for those wanting tours, for the curious, for those interested in the jobs on offer, for locals and tourists alike. News of the ship's arrival has spread far and wide and Porlock Weir was once again rammed with onlookers, all keen to witness the remarkable vessel anchored in the bay. A constant stream of rowing boats and dinghies helped with the transportation, their owners enjoying the continuing festive atmosphere while making a few pennies that would be spent in the pub later. Ramon and his crew had provided snacks and drinks, the ship was gleaming, smelling of fresh wood, tar, canvas and new ropes, and festooned with bunting. Everyone was in good humour.

To all who came on board, Ramon introduced the members of the crew: his younger sister Elisa, 40s, unmarried ('Some say untamed'), along for the adventure; his captain Sebastian known as Seb, late 60s, a seasoned sailor ('Happiest with a beer in his hand'); the cook Cassandra, Greek, 50s, fiery ('Keep out of the galley when she's busy'); and the ten young Spanish crew members, all male, all cocky, all enjoying the adventure too. 'They're a good bunch of boys,' Ramon explained, 'but they don't speak much English.'

For the local inhabitants, Ramon's arrival speech had raised countless questions. He'd fielded many of these tactfully when he'd mingled with the crowd the previous day and so was fully prepared to receive another bombardment now. Intrigued by this handsome Spaniard, he was approached throughout the day by inquisitive individuals and groups, all keen to learn more.

Ramon was, they learned, a wealthy married industrialist who had built up a successful high-end construction business in the south of Spain. Born and raised by the sea, he had a natural passion for sailing and so, reaching the age of about 50 and with a healthy bank balance, he decided to revert to the traditional family business and bought a shipyard in Seville where he started specialising in historical replicas. The family remembered his great-grandparents' promise and they started building the Porlock Maria a couple of years ago. The construction remained a close secret as he wanted it to be a surprise for the people of Porlock.

Although the exterior of the ship was accurate historically, the below decks had been built for the 21st century – plush cabins, modern showers, a sleek kitchen, an ample mess, a well-stocked bar, a comfortable lounge, and every other convenience. It was only the captain's quarters that had been fitted out in a more traditional style and this was where Seb spent much of the day, interviewing the dozens of hopefuls who'd come aboard to enquire about the jobs. One by one, the men and women of varying ages chatted with the captain, all enthused by the golden opportunity to become involved in such an exciting adventure, to travel the oceans and seas of the world, to gain sea-faring experience, to open doors to endless new possibilities.

The position of the new captain had to go to somebody with extensive experience and so this vacancy had already been filled – the ex-harbour master of Porlock Weir, Salty, who'd been approached several weeks previously. Other roles that needed filling included chief medical officer, cook, carpenter, electrician, plumber, engineer, bo'sun and general deckhands, and every crew member would be trained to cover other roles too. Most of the new crew would be required on a part-time basis only, for up to six to eight months a year when the ship would be travelling, leaving only the captain and two others to live on the ship permanently when it was anchored at Porlock Weir.

By late in the afternoon, Seb had interviewed all the candidates and was close to a decision. He had been given only two weeks to choose the new crew and get them trained and so those with some ship experience and the necessary trade skills were the front-runners. He had a brief meeting with Ramon and they agreed that, after further discussions later in the day, they'd invite the successful applicants on board the following morning and start some introductory training. Over the next fortnight, the training would include a few short trips in the vicinity of Porlock Bay but the first real test for the new crew would be a journey up the channel to Bristol, to show off and publicise the Porlock Maria on her first official voyage.

***

Meanwhile, up on deck, a special additional festivity for the visitors was being prepared. A rowing boat had been lowered and, powered by two oarsmen, headed towards the open channel towing a faded and semi-ruinous dinghy containing a pile of cloth. At a distance of about 150 metres from the ship, they paused. One of the oarsmen hopped agilely into the dilapidated dinghy, dropped a small anchor and spent a few minutes manipulating the cloth until, eventually, what appeared to be a man was sitting upright. The figure was wearing the mask and a costume of a pirate, it appeared, onto which a tricorn hat was placed. The crew member stepped back into the rowing boat and untied the connecting rope before making their way slowly back to the ship.

By this time, their antics had attracted the curiosity of all remaining 20 or so visitors, including Pete who'd come aboard later in the day to avoid the earlier rush. Drinks in hand as the lazy sun started to dip in the sky, everyone watched the boat peacefully return until they were joined by Ramon on the deck.

'My good friends,' he began loudly as they turned to face him. 'I hope you've all had a pleasant stay on the ship on this lovely afternoon.' Agreement, nods and smiles from all.

'I have one more surprise for you,' he continued. 'It is something that I hope you will enjoy and that you may like to try. We have had special permission from the harbour master to put on a little display of target practice, starting in a few minutes.'

A brief pause before Ramon gestured towards the four small brass cannons that lined the starboard side that faced the open sea and where they were all assembled.

'You heard the cannons yesterday but we fired blanks only. Today we fire real shot! In a few moments, we will aim our cannons at that little boat out in the bay and try to hit it. And, if you like, you can all have a go too!'

Delight, surprise and a few worried looks from the small gathering and so Ramon continued.

'To explain a bit more so that you are all happy,' he said. 'The balls that we will be using are not real cannon balls but just old plastic buoys that we brought with us. In the little boat that you see, there is a pirate, the most wicked of men, that we must try to hit. The balls will also not sink as they are buoys but the boat may not survive. After we have finished, we will collect the boat and the buoys so that we can have fun again at another time!'

Ramon and Elisa distributed earplugs, the crew members took up their positions by the cannons, uncovered the stacks of small orange buoys and powder kegs and started loading.

'My crew will fire a few first,' Ramon explained, 'to find their range and show you how it's done, then you can try.'

Gunpowder loaded, wadding and balls rammed down, ropes tightened, aim taken, spectators well
back, and a quick safety check by Seb. Happy with everything, the captain raised his arm, scanned the gun crews one last time, and then brought his arm swiftly down. The noise on deck was deafening – shrieks and oaths from many as the cannons rocked back, unleashing long plumes of grey smoke and sending the balls

hurtling across the bay. After only a few seconds, impressive splashes could be seen – two that fell short, one too long and one just to the right of the dinghy.

Accompanied by exhilarated cheers and whoops, two more practice shots followed from each cannon before the visitors had their chance. After small adjustments and a few direct hits, the battered dinghy in the bay could still be seen afloat although the pirate had been obliterated early on by Marjorie, the President of the local Women's Institute. The sea around the boat was strewn with shredded rubber, torn cloth and floating orange balls.

After all 40 balls had been fired, the entertainment was over. The rowing boat went out to collect the balls and the debris and, as Pete languidly watched it return, he noticed the Spanish woman further down the deck, similarly alone and looking out to sea. Attractive, in jeans and t-shirt and with her long dark hair loose, Pete couldn't resist. A glass of wine in hand, he ambled over, smoothing his hair as he went and fixing his best smile.

'A very impressive and enjoyable show,' he said as he leant on the polished wooden railing next to Elisa, turning his head towards her.

She looked at him quizzically with a small smile. 'It was,' she replied with a strong accent. 'It was my brother Ramon's idea. To make friends in Porlock, he said.'

'He's done that very well already,' said Pete. 'You all have. Your visit, the ship, caught us all by surprise – all most impressive. Nobody can quite believe all of this. Your generosity is astounding. I assume that you were in contact with some people here, to make all the arrangements?'

'Ah,' said Elisa, 'others have asked the same of me. But I, like my brother, cannot say anything. I have not been much involved anyway. Ramon has done everything.'

'I understand,' replied Pete. 'But, if you don't mind me asking, why are you here? It's wonderful that you have come, of course, but do you have a job on the ship too?'

She smiled and looked at him. 'No,' she said. 'I am only a passenger, along for the ride, I think you say. Ramon has talked about the trip to Porlock for many months. It sounded exciting, I like the sea and my family history and so Ramon let me come along.'

'So no ties at home, no work, no family?' Pete asked hopefully.

'Not at the moment,' she replied. 'I am, how do you say, a free woman. I do some work sometimes for Ramon and he looks after me. Most of the time, I do what I want.'

They continued to chat for a short while and introductions were made. Pete mentioned in passing his distant Spanish ancestry and his youthful passion for the Mediterranean, while Elisa talked vaguely about her carefree lifestyle, travelling the world and happy on her own.

Pete, starting to warm to this kindred spirit, offered to get her a drink. As he returned and passed her a glass of wine, she noticed a ring on his hand - dulled gold, a blood-red stone setting, seemingly antique.

'That is an unusual ring you have,' she commented.

'I've only just started wearing it,' Pete replied. 'It's an old love charm apparently. It belongs to my mother. Thought I'd see if it worked.'

'You never know,' Elisa replied, studying the ring more closely. 'I do not believe in that sort of thing but it's a strange world.'

'It's an attractive ring all the same,' said Pete. 'And,' he continued with a twinkle in his eye, 'it caught the attention of a beautiful woman like you.'

A loud laugh from Elisa followed by a tut or two and a mock slap of the face, and the two, giggling, finished their wines and went off together in search of top-ups.

Six o'clock and a couple more wines enjoyed, the two lounged side by side in canvas chairs on the top deck, watching the sun starting to set and guests gradually departing to shore. The conversation swung slowly from chit-chat to the more personal, as each learned more about the other, their stories, their desires, their hopes, lives and loves. Pete, a seasoned courter, found himself increasingly intrigued and captivated by this unusual and confident woman, the fact that she was very attractive being a delightful bonus.

As the sun eventually dipped, Pete thanked Ramon and the crew members for the enjoyable day before heading towards the ladder. His last farewell, with a small kiss on the cheek, was to Elisa.

'Remember,' he told her as he started to climb down to the boat. 'The Bottom Ship tomorrow night, seven o'clock. I'm buying.'

A coy smile and small wave. 'Looking forward to it.'

9

The village was alive with the bustle of a summer Monday. By midday, the shops were busy, the pavements crowded, the High Street a constant stream of cars, bikes, coaches, caravans, all on their holiday journeys to the seaside, the moor, further west or, on this particular day, down to Porlock Weir to witness for themselves the galleon that everyone was talking about.

Casual visitors meandered leisurely through the quiet back lanes and alleys of Porlock, admiring the history, the thatch, the tradition, the understated antiquity of the place, cameras in hand and greeting each other courteously as they crossed paths. In the gentle flow, three men wove their individual ways from various edges of the village, all heading in the same direction at the same time. Nobody paid them any attention. Approaching the back of the High Street, each found the worn old door to the small enclosed yard and, one after the other, they entered.

The kettle had just boiled when knocks on the back door announced the arrival of the guests. Joe hustled them into the back room of his shop, a familiar and common meeting place. The smell wasn't great but the back rooms of butcher's shops rarely smelled fragrant. The tired walls were covered with old posters of farm auctions, photographs of young hopefuls receiving cups and awards at agricultural shows, and many tatty certificates of achievement, for Joe and his family, spanning the last 50 years or more. In his 60s now, Joe was third generation butcher, Exmoor born and bred, and as stocky as a Red Devon bull. Ruddy-faced and bald, he was a distinctive and popular character in the area, mild of manner and thoughtful.

Polite as ever, Joe took off his stained apron and sat his guests down around the table, offering teas and coffees. The sink in the corner needed a scrub, the stone floor hadn't been swept in a while, but everything else was passable. The spoons on the rickety oak table were at least clean.

'It hasn't changed much,' noted Bob, looking around.

'No, not much since you were last here,' replied Joe. 'Must be about 20 years ago, at least. It's a shame you didn't want to stay – you were a good butcher. Could have made a career out of it.'

'Thanks, but the undertaking trade suited me better,' said Bob. 'Janey's always said I was happiest dealing with bodies that didn't answer back.'

'I know what you mean,' smiled Joe. 'The conversations would be a bit one-sided.'

The three men sat down at the table while Joe prepared the beverages.

'Thanks for coming at such short notice,' he began as he started passing around the mugs. 'I was told you all received notes last night asking for your help. I got one too and it also said to get you lot in here today to talk and compare notes, so to speak. We can't be too long as I'm on my lunch break.'

All four men had lived in Porlock Vale for most, if not all, of their lives. All were respected, knowledgeable, forthright and trustworthy: Colin, Bob the Box, Joe and the eldest, Fred The Forge, former blacksmith and a 'document technician' as he liked to call himself. All notes mentioned the South African, Bram de Jong. All notes also mentioned that he was actively seeking to obstruct the successful foundation of the new Porlock Maria venture and their help was being requested.

Colin started. 'I always thought he was hiding something and now we know what it is. Must be why he turned up exactly when the ship arrived. Oh, and Vince told me he did some checking on the internet and there's no record of a Bram de Jong at Pretoria University, past or present. Very dodgy chap, it seems. I'm more than happy to help.'

'So what did your note say?' asked Joe.

'It asked me to work with Fred, who will give me some papers that I should give to Bram, and tell him that I found them in the museum archive.'

'That's what my note said too, more or less,' said Fred. 'It asked me to produce a few old scraps of paper, with a few lines of hand-written verse in the style of Coleridge. Imitating Coleridge's hand-writing as well, if I can find any samples of that. It says to then give them to you, Colin, who can help me with the style as you know more about it than I do.'

'I'm happy to,' replied Colin. 'It sounds a bit suspect, though.'

'Don't worry about that,' Fred reassured him. 'Just tell him you found them and they appear to be Coleridge's style and in his hand but there's no proof. Let him draw his own conclusions.'

'Well,' said Colin, 'putting it like that, I suppose it's okay.'

'I'm not so sure either,' Joe said quietly. 'I haven't met this bloke yet but, from what you've all told me, I can't see anything wrong. You say he's got a strange manner and has been asking some unusual questions, but what's wrong with that? I was happy to help with the barbecue when the ship arrived but this new request – well, it doesn't sit quite right with me.'

'I know these requests sounds odd,' replied Bob, 'but I'm sure it's all for a very good reason. Do you remember, must be eight or so years ago, when we were all asked to help block that application for a supermarket up the hill? We all worked together, used our contacts, and we won. That turned out well. The land's protected forever now, thanks to the money given by an anonymous donor.'

'And that awful by-pass project that was going to cut across the moor,' Colin mentioned. 'The same sort of thing.'

'Even longer ago,' Fred joined in, 'we had to fight to get a fire brigade here. I remember a substantial anonymous donation then that swung it in our favour. That was a good day for the village.'

Joe took a considered sip from his mug. 'I remember all of those,' he said, 'and you're right, they all turned out well.'

'So,' Bob went, 'it's the same now. We might not know all the reasons why we're asked to help but we do know it's for a very good cause and we wouldn't be asked to help out unless it was necessary. I for one am willing to help.'

Fred and Colin both nodded earnestly in agreement, and looked to Joe.

'All right, you've persuaded me,' he said at last. 'If this South African bloke is just a tourist, hopefully no harm will be done. As long as I don't get mixed up in anything dodgy, I'm happy to help too.'

'And if he's not on the level,' Bob replied, 'we'll have helped to stop whatever he's up to. This Porlock Maria thing could be huge for us all and, if this bloke is trying to scupper the venture somehow, we have to help stop him. Agreed?'

The others muttered their agreement.

After a few thoughtful moments, Colin turned to Fred. 'So, Fred, about these papers you've been asked to make,' he started. 'I should be able to write some verse in Coleridge's style. About anything in particular, do you know?'

'Ah,' Fred replied, looking down at the note which he'd taken from his pocket. 'It says, one verse needs to say something like '*caverns of dragon gold measureless to man*' and another verse something like '*a pixie path and sacred stones, the prize deep in a haunted glade*,' whatever that means.'

'That ties in with what I've been asked to do,' said Bob. 'You know that old smuggling cave up the coast, almost completely blocked off now, on Jack's land? Well, I've been asked to show Bram where it is, if he asks. And to give him a torch with batteries that are nearly dead. The note says talk to all of you, especially Joe.'

'I was asked just to talk with you lot,' said Joe, 'and also give Bob a sackful of old bones from the shop. I've got plenty of those. He says you'll know what to do with them, Bob.'

'I think I have an idea,' replied Bob thoughtfully.

'When I chatted with Bram a few days ago,' Colin said, 'I think I mentioned your name, Bob. He was asking about caves and I told him that you know about these things, being from an old smuggling family. And he said it was connected with his research on Coleridge.'

'Okay,' replied Bob, 'this is starting to make more sense now. It looks as if we're all being asked to set up this South African and lure him to the old cave. Colin, if he mentions the cave again, tell him to talk to me. But, after he's there, what then? Has anybody been asked to do anything else?'

'Not me,' replied Joe. 'At least, not yet.'

'Nor me,' said both Fred and Colin.

'We're up against a deadline, though', Fred went on. 'I've been asked to get the papers done by tomorrow morning. Tight but I can do it – with your help, Colin.'

'Of course,' said Colin with a smile. 'We'll have a chat separately after this. Looks as if this Bram problem needs to be sorted quickly. Time to get weaving, chaps.'

They all finished their cups and made arrangements to meet up again soon. Joe returned to his shop and the others slipped out, quietly and unseen, by the back door.

10

From Monday onwards, the ship was closed to visitors. Even so, the harbourside was busy, its shops enjoying a bumper trade in coffees, ice creams, fudge and Porlock Maria souvenir badges that had somehow appeared overnight. Another sunny day of lounging around, picnics on the beach, kids paddling and crabbing, beers at the pub, yachts swerving lazily in the bay, gulls calling and lukewarm pasties.

At the quay, all 30 successful applicants had arrived promptly. All keen, all excited, they were efficiently transferred on board where they gathered in a group on the deck. Of both sexes and ranging in age from 17 to 42, most knew each other and all understood that they'd been selected for their particular skills, maritime experience, fitness, character and their ability to start the training immediately without impacting other responsibilities. Several deckhands put them at their ease and, once they'd all settled, the veteran captain emerged from his cabin, followed by the various other members of the crew with the exception of Ramon and Elisa. Seb, unshaven and burly, scanned the new recruits intensely as the rest of his crew stood behind him, and then ran through the introduction.

The training, he explained in good English, was to last two weeks although, after the first week the 30 applicants would be reduced to only 11, the final new crew. During the first week, they would all be trained in their preferred job on the ship as well as a back-up in another role. As he appreciated that they may have other responsibilities at the moment, everyone must train for a minimum of four days in the first week. After the first week, the final 11 will be given intensive training for five days. This time should be adequate as the current crew would return to Spain then although, if more basic training is needed, some members of the current crew may stay on briefly. The new captain and bo'sun would be responsible for all training on-going.

Everyone would also be trained on basic seamanship which included ship handling and navigation, route planning, ropes and sails, anchoring and docking, maritime law, health and safety, emergency procedures and general duties.

'This is no holiday,' Seb reiterated sternly. 'The next two weeks will be hard work but, for those of you who are chosen, it will be worth it, I promise.'

All the recruits appeared undaunted by the demanding schedule. Among the group were Mark and a few of his friends, Sid, Ron, Spike and Harry, all with different skills and all willing to grasp this opportunity to expand their horizons. Mark, Spike and Ron applied for the posts of Chief Carpenter, Plumber and Electrician respectively while Sid and Harry, young, strong and experienced sailors, hoped to become deckhands.

After a short time with paperwork, Seb gave the applicants one hour to tour the ship at their leisure, to inspect their working areas and equipment, to talk to the crew, to become familiar with their potential home for several months at a time. After this, a light lunch and then the start of the training.

Mark, Spike and the other hopeful carpenters and plumbers were accompanied by Pablo and Carlos, both enthusiastic young deckhands clearly enjoying the adventure. The viewing of the ship finished and with a little time on their hands, Mark and Spike had a chance to chat to the Spaniards and the subject of the triathlon on Saturday came up.

'I want to do it,' said Carlos eagerly after Mark had explained what was involved. 'I am strong and I can ride. I can win, I know!'

'I'm sorry, Carlos, but it's not as easy as that,' Mark said. 'You can only take part if you live here.'

'But I live here for two weeks,' Carlos replied keenly. 'I like running and boating too. I will have fun. And Pablo, he wants to do it too, yes Pablo?'

'Si, me too,' said Pablo, the younger of the two, dark curly hair and infectious smile.

'But I'm not sure…' Mark started, until he saw the growing look of disappointment on their faces.

'Tell you what,' interrupted Spike. 'We'll find out if anything can be done. I mean, you don't live here but you lot, on the ship, have done such a good thing for Porlock and for us, the people in charge of the event might allow you to join in. A gesture of goodwill, if you like.'

'Good idea, mate,' replied Mark. 'It can't hurt to ask, can it? We'll see what we can do.'

Carlos' and Pablo's faces lit up with clear delight, followed by warm hugs and many 'Gracias, amigos'.

Mark and Spike were about to move off to look around the ship a bit more on their own, when Mark was stopped by a worried looking Pablo.

'Excuse me, Mark,' he began. 'My English is not good but I am afraid of…sharks. Is that the right word?'

When Mark nodded, Pablo continued. 'I don't like sharks. You have sharks in the sea here?'

'No,' replied Mark with a smile, 'nothing like that. You can swim safely here, don't worry.'

'Well,' said Spike with a mischievous smile and wink to Mark, 'there is a legend of a sea monster that lives here, a big fierce serpent that drags ships down to the depths, but I haven't seen it myself.'

After translation by Carlos, Pablo's face switched from puzzlement to trepidation, followed by animated chatter between the two as Mark and Spike walked away, chuckling.

The enticing smell of cooking lured the men below deck and towards the galley where they saw a short aproned woman with tangled black hair tied back attending the two sizzling hobs and scooping small snacks onto platters, assisted by a younger man, both oblivious at first to their arrival. The change in light from the doorway alerted the cook to their presence and, turning and looking them up and down, she addressed them.

'You the new recruits?' They nodded. 'Good. Just in time to help us. We serve lunch in five minutes.'

They awkwardly introduced themselves as the others bustled to prepare.

'I am Cassandra, call me Cass,' the woman volunteered as she continued working. 'I am from Greece, where the best food in the world comes from. If you don't know that now, you will soon.'

She flashed them a quick smile before returning to her hobs and oven. After a few minutes, several bowls, platters and baskets had been filled and were ready to go out. Together with Teo, Cass' assistant, the men took the dishes up on deck where the tables had been prepared for the buffet lunch, and then returned to help further. After a few more trips, with most of the lunch taken up, Mark remained in the galley with Cass as the final two platters were ready to go.

'There,' said Cass with satisfaction. 'I am happy with that. Thank you for your help.'

'No problem,' replied Mark.

Cass looked Mark up and down again. 'You are a big man,' she said admiringly, 'and strong, I see. I hope you don't want to work in the galley. You will not fit easily in here.'

'Carpenter,' smiled Mark, 'though I enjoy cooking. Your food looks and smells wonderful. My mother's a good cook too, likes baking. She makes cakes and sells them in the bakery in Porlock.'

'Ah,' said Cass, wiping her brow, taking off her apron and looking at Mark intently with black eyes. 'I think I met her on Saturday, at the party when we arrived. I went on shore and tried a cake. It was very good.'

'They're the best,' agreed Mark. 'She wants to start her own cake shop in Porlock Weir as soon as she gets enough money.'

'That sounds like a good plan,' smiled Cass encouragingly. 'I look forward to meeting her again. I am happy to try her cakes once more and help her in any way I can.

'Now,' she continued, handing Mark the last platters. 'Take these up. It is time for lunch and I am hungry. I also need a glass of wine.'

**

Later the same day, up in Porlock, two friends sat down in a café for a pot of tea and some cake. It was a café that they'd both frequented before, together and with other friends too, and so nothing looked suspicious. Since Saturday, gossip and rumours seemed to be the sole topic of conversation in the village but, as the novelty of the ship's arrival slowly waned and there were no apparent unwarranted and awkward questions from outside authorities, the two decided that their meetings could now be slightly less covert. After all, with the exception of one remaining risk, their part in the game was almost over.

The cafe was not full but, even so, they chose a corner table away from others. Waiting for the tea and cake to arrive, they chatted cheerfully as usual in public, noting that only a couple of casual acquaintances were also there, reducing the risk of interruption. Once the waitress had left, they lowered their voices and, ever vigilant, got to the purpose.

M: 'Everyone's received their instructions and, I hope, they'll all do as they've been asked.'

T: 'That's good. We can't afford for the plan not to work. It's risky, of course, but he has to go – there's too much at stake.'

M: 'So, once he's lured to the cave, are you sure we don't want to involve anybody else?'

T: 'I'm sure. If something goes wrong, we don't want anybody else involved. It should be safe enough but accidents can happen.'

M: 'I'm happy with that. I'll need the old figurehead very soon, though, so I have a chance to do it up and then put it in place. Can you get it for me later today?'

T: 'I've got a set of keys to the pantomime store so I'll get it out tonight. It's been there gathering dust for at least seven years. That Viking panto was one of the best and the ship was the star of the show, I remember. The dragon head's all that's left now. The last time I saw it, it was very faded and so it'll need a bit of paint added as well as the horns. Make it look like the devil incarnate if you can.'

M: 'I'll do my best. If you get it to me by tomorrow morning, I'll have it ready by the end of tomorrow and I'll put it in place Wednesday morning before the sun rises.'

T: 'Great, thanks. If he takes the bait, we don't know when he'll go so we need to be ready as soon as possible. You sure you don't need any help? The figurehead's quite heavy and it'll be difficult to manoeuvre in the cave.'

M: 'I'll manage. I'll take it by boat. I know my way in and I'll be careful. I'll put it over the old shaft to the sea so it blocks the light, and prop it up with stones.'

T: 'It'll look just like the devil in the right light. I hear he's afraid of the devil so hopefully he'll scarper.'

M: 'If he doesn't, it's very dangerous in the cave, loose and slippery stones everywhere. Only one tight entrance and exit. If he did have an accident, a rockfall for example, he may never be found.'

T: 'Well, that would be unfortunate, of course. Let's hope our scare tactics work. If it doesn't, we'll implement plan B. If that fails, plan C but I don't want to think about that yet.'

M: 'You mean…?'

T: 'We have to be prepared to do whatever we have to, to protect the secret. You know that. We've been lucky that it hasn't been necessary in our time. But you know the story about the woodcutter?'

M: 'I remember. He was a guardian who tried to take all the gold and was found in his store in the same state as his wood. Didn't your father tell you that story?'

T: 'Yes, when he passed over the guardianship to me. It happened back in the 1940s, he said. A true story as well – I read about it in the museum archives although it was reported just as a common murder. They didn't find the culprit, of course.'

M: 'Let's hope we don't have to go to those lengths with Bram.'

T: 'I'm sure we can put him off some other way. We can't let him find out.'

M: 'This all assumes that he is a treasure-hunter and onto us. If he's legitimate, he'll run.'

T: 'We'll know soon enough. A real Coleridge academic will spot the forged papers in an instant. If he's genuine, we'll call the whole thing off. If he's a fraud, he deserves everything coming to him.'

11

The turf trembled as the horses thudded past at full gallop. Colin stepped back well out of the way as his camera panned and clicked multiple times, the high shutter speed freezing the images of the beasts heading across the field in clouds of dust. The moor in the background and the late afternoon sun tinting the wisps of thin low clouds with gold. Colin was happy.

The training ground at Vic's farm had been quiet in the morning when most of those taking advantage of the free riding practice were at work or otherwise occupied. Four o'clock usually marked the beginning of the rush and so Anne ensured that all her horses had been fully rested and ready. Most of them would be used in the event, for those without their own horses. Many entrants already had their own or could borrow from elsewhere and Anne was happy to allow them to practice on her two-mile training circuit. Her staff were on hand to help and advise, her father Vic stopped by occasionally to view the progress and her brother Dan was there to help too if needed. It was Tuesday - only four more days until the triathlon.

Old friends Raymond, George, Jack and John watched with interest. It was going to be the biggest local event for many years and they all knew most of the competitors - young men and women born and bred in the Vale, some of them relatives, many involved in the farming life, the next generation all keen to perform well. As they were discussing the various merits of the youngsters, the pros and cons, Vic walked over with an armful of cold bottled beers from his Land Rover.

'Well, boys,' he said as he passed around the bottles, 'who's your favourite? They all look promising but it's going to be a close call. I'm not getting my money out yet.'

'No rush,' replied Raymond. 'The sweepstake's open until Friday night. Is £50 each still okay with everyone?'

They all murmured their agreement.

'Good, thanks,' said Raymond. 'A bottle of good single malt if anyone picks the winner and the rest of the money into the pot for the youngsters.'

Crunching up the track and stopping by the stables was a familiar old blue pick-up.

All doors opened, Mark stepping out of the driver's side, Spike and Ron from the front passenger side and, spilling out of the confined rear seats, four young dark swarthy men. A few heads turned to view the arrival of the strangers who, once Mark had had a quick word with them, followed him to where the older farmers were grouped.

'Vic,' Mark said cheerfully as they approached. 'Ship training's finished for the day so I thought we'd all come up here for some more practice. These are the Spanish boys I told you about – Teo, Pablo, Fabio and Carlos.'

Greetings, handshakes and other introductions over, Carlos, with a little bow to Vic, began his prepared speech.

'We would all like to say thank you, señor Vic, for allowing us to do the games. We are very happy to be here in beautiful Porlock and to help your friends. It is an honour for us.'

Vic smiled. 'It's my pleasure,' he said, 'and thank you for the words. Mark called me and explained. As you're helping us all out so much, I'm only too happy for you to join in the triathlon. I assume Mark told you about the prizes?'

'I've told them,' replied Mark. 'They know the prize money is for locals only but they're happy to join in just for the fun of it anyway.'

'Good luck with it, Mark,' said Jack. 'My money's on you so you better do well. I reckon you'll storm the riding bit and you're in good trim at the moment. Must be all that rugby you play.'

'I'll do my best', replied Mark with a wry smile. 'I'm built for a number eight, okay on the field but not distance running, so I'm a bit worried about that part. I reckon our new friends here will do well, they're all strong and athletic.'

The Spaniards, more or less understanding the gist of the conversation, pumped up their chests and flexed a few muscles, comically mock heroic, as the others chuckled. 'Si,' said Fabio, 'we are strong!'

A few more cars and four-by-fours, some with horseboxes, had arrived and the yard was busy. The event was only a few days away and, although the atmosphere was ostensibly light and cheery, the training was becoming more serious, more tense, as the competitors, some huddled in small groups, assessed their rivals. The triathlon was not for the faint-hearted and the prize money was substantial. Everyone was gunning for the top prize.

Vic had wandered off back to the house, John and Jack were looking at the horses in the stables, leaving Raymond and George, two veteran farmers, enjoying the sight of the horses pounding across the fields. They'd just opened another beer from the box that Vic had left with them when they were joined by Colin, his camera back in his bag.

'I'm taking a rest from the photos, think I've got some good ones' explained Colin, viewing the fields. 'Lots of people here this afternoon. All locals, apart from those Spanish boys from the ship.'

'Yes,' replied Raymond. 'A good turn-out. Those Spanish lads are doing well, good riders. There was another foreigner up here this afternoon, says he knows you. South African.'

'Oh, yes?' asked Colin, interest piqued.

'Nice enough bloke,' continued Raymond, 'called Bram. Says he heard about the training here, thought he'd come and have a look, if Vic doesn't mind. Vic was here and said it's fine.'

'I've bumped into him once or twice,' admitted Colin cautiously. 'On holiday. Did he ask you anything?'

'General chit-chat, about the triathlon, the ship and stuff. He praised Rik and Vic for sponsoring the event and then mentioned something about the money the ship must have cost. He was asking strange questions almost as if he thought we knew something about it.'

'He was a funny character,' said George. 'We just laughed when he mentioned the cost of the ship. I mean, that Spanish bloke, Ramon, paid for the ship, didn't he? I know our families help out the village from time to time but we've got nothing to do with this and don't have that sort of money anyway.'

'Yes', mused Colin, 'he is odd. He's an academic, doing some research, so he's used to asking unusual questions, I suppose. But, yes, very odd.'

The afternoon stretched into early evening and most started to drift homewards. Anne was keeping the facilities open until six o'clock and so Colin hung around on the off-chance of more photos while the farmers loitered too, enticed by cakes and tea provided by Vic's wife, Mags. Mark herded his friends and the Spaniards back into the pick-up and set off back down the rubbly track, passing Joe's butcher's van on his way up with the weekly delivery.

Once Joe had dropped off the boxes with Mags, he wandered over to the stables to watch the last horses coming and going and saw Colin there, long lens focused on the distant circuit. Nobody else was close and so the two men briefly compared notes.

'So how did it go, Colin,' Joe asked, 'with Fred's bits of paper?'

'Surprisingly well. Fred was fantastic and gave them to me this morning. He'd used real ink on faded paper, looked very authentic. He said he found examples of Coleridge's handwriting online and tried to imitate it as best he could in the time he had. So I phoned Bram who wanted to see them straight away. Met him in the café earlier.'

'And what did he make of them?'

'Totally fooled!' Colin replied with a smile. 'I spun him the story, mentioned they looked like drafts of Kubla Khan, including an unfinished part, and he fell for it. He didn't check the writing or ask any other questions, just got very excited and then asked about the caves again, especially the one with the devil legend, said he'd love to take a look. So I said I'd put him in touch with Bob, as we said.'

'Did he ask anything else?' asked Joe.

'He asked if the caves were close to the farm where Coleridge wrote Kubla Khan, and I said they were. Oh, and he also asked if the 'haunted glade' in Fred's papers meant anything to me. I said that there is an old wood up the hill that's meant to be haunted, near some standing stones, that nobody ever dares to enter. Bram said he'd love to see that too – archaeological interest, he said.'

'Whatever he's up to, he's very keen,' said Joe. 'It sounds a bit suspicious.'

'I agree,' replied Colin. 'He was up here earlier today too. He was asking George and Raymond about the ship, a lot of strange questions. I'm convinced now that he isn't what he claims to be – he didn't even spot that Fred's papers were forgeries!'

'Let's all carry on and do as we've been asked, then,' said Joe. 'I've given loads of bones to Bob and am happy to do anything else that's asked of me. Hopefully this problem, whatever it is, will get sorted soon.'

Joe returned to his van as the place started to empty. Anne and her staff were bringing in and grooming the tired horses, Dan was helping to tidy and Vic and his friends had disappeared. Colin packed up his camera gear and went in search of a toilet before he departed. Not knowing the farm well, he went to the main house, found an open door to the kitchen at the rear and, with nobody there to ask, tentatively went in. There was a closed door to the right that looked promising and, as he was just about to open it, he heard muffled voices from the other side. Not wishing to intrude, he was just about to turn away when he heard a few indistinct phrases that caught his attention.

Two voices, both male, talking quietly, local accents - '...got to do it...', '...for the future of Porlock...', '...nobody can know it's our decision...', '...for the best...'

The voices were barely audible and yet Colin thought that he recognised one. Just as he was about to put his ear to the door to hear more, a loud 'Can I help you?' from behind startled him. Turning to see a puzzled Dan in the doorway, Colin quickly composed himself, explained his predicament with the toilet, and was duly guided in the right direction.

Back in his car, Colin pondered. That voice was very familiar but he couldn't quite place it. He'd sleep on it and, by the morning, he was sure he would know.

12

They had to work fast but everything was in place in time. Bram had contacted Colin in the morning, asking again to visit the caves as soon as possible, then Colin had contacted Bob who confirmed that he was ready. Checks with the others as well – thumbs up all around. They arranged for Colin to bring Bram up to Jack's farm that afternoon at two o'clock.

They arrived dead on time. As they pulled into Jack's yard, Bob was already waiting, wearing worn camouflage clothing and holding a tatty rucksack. Next to him stood the imposing figures of Jack, Raymond and Vic, all standing outside Jack's woodworking shed, all clasping small bundles of paper, and all watching the arrival in silence.

Once out of the car and introductions over, Colin looked querulously at the paper that the three men were holding.

'Oh, we're just practicing my lines,' Jack explained. 'Vic and Raymond came over for a chat and were happy to help. Vic is reading the Captain Hook lines, Raymond the Peter Pan ones and I'm Smee of course.'

'Very different to farming,' noted Bram.

'Yes,' replied Vic, watching Bram. 'It's a good distraction from farming.'

'We enjoy the disguises,' Jack said, watching Bram too. 'Pretending to be other characters. You must know what we mean.'

Bram looked up at Jack. 'I'm not sure what you mean,' he replied slowly.

'It's just that you have the bearing of an actor,' Jack continued. 'You know, tall, confident. So you've never done any acting?'

'No, none,' Bram replied carefully, 'except at school a long time ago, of course.'

A brief pause as the men looked at one another, and then Bob cut in. 'I don't like to interrupt but we have to get moving soon. The tide.'

'Of course,' said Jack, stepping back. 'We'll let you get on.'

'So, Bram, what exactly are you looking for?' asked Raymond before they could start on their way. 'Bob said you're researching Coleridge.'

'That's right,' Bram replied, happy to be back on safer ground. 'I believe this cave may have inspired Coleridge to write his Kubla Khan poem. I'm just interested in visiting historic places, for my research.'

'There's nothing down there now,' said Jack. 'I haven't been in for years but, when I did, it was just a wet cave. Very slippery and probably quite dangerous now. And spooky too, if you believe the legend.'

'I heard about that,' Bram replied. 'The devil dragging you down. I'll risk it.'

'Be careful,' Vic warned. 'This is an old place with old memories. Plenty of stories of the devil, ghosts and the like here. It's a dangerous place to get lost. But I'm sure you'll be fine. Bob here will help you, knows the place like the back of his hand.'

'I don't want any accidents on my land,' Jack said. 'Bob, Colin, look after our guest. When you're done, come back here and I'll put the kettle on.'

Gear and clothing checked, the three men said their farewells and ambled away from the farm. Jack, Vic and Raymond watched them with interest before returning into the confines of the shed.

Bob led the way, followed by Colin and Bram, all chatting amiably as they went. Up the lane, through a gate, across two fields, downhill, through another gate, into the ancient woods, then picking up a tight deer track that descended ever more steeply towards the cliffs and the gently swishing sea.

The vegetation became more thick and tangled, spikes and twigs clawing at their trousers, yet Bob seemed to know his way. The whoosh of the sea not far away. A startled deer, a few squawking pheasants, darting rabbits and curious squirrels were the only witnesses to their progress through dense undergrowth well away from established footpaths. More steeply now, the sound of waves crashing on rocks close by, down a zig-zag path that suddenly seemed to stop.

'This is it,' said Bob as the others looked around in puzzlement. Bob smiled, put on a pair of gloves and pulled aside a dense bush of brambles to reveal slabs of roughly-hewn stone in the middle of which was a circular and mossy hole no more than a few feet wide. On one edge could be seen rusted iron rivets that may have once secured a wooden cover, long since reclaimed by the elements and, within the hole, the darkness of the void.

'Right, Bram,' said Bob, handing him a torch from the rucksack. 'You'll need this. Just in that hole you'll find some stone steps, a bit slippery and uneven but solid. There's no hand-holds anymore so go carefully. The steps will go down about 20 feet, then turn right, down another 20 or so, then left. You should hear the sea quite loudly at about that point. Go down a bit further and you'll come to the cave.'

Bram looked a little worried. 'So, you're sure you don't want to come down with me?' he asked.

'Not a chance,' replied Bob. 'As I told you, it's very slippery and I'm not as young as I used to be. And there's the legend of the devil that lives there too but I've never seen it. No, I'm staying here with Colin. If you want to go in, you're on your own.'

Bram paused, as if about to change his mind, but then looked resolute once again. 'I must admit, I am superstitious and so I'm nervous. I'm sure the devil isn't really down there but it's the condition of the place I'm more worried about. Are you sure it's safe?'

'I haven't been inside for a few years,' lied Bob, 'but it was solid enough when I went in last time. There'll be loose rocks and you'll see the old gap through the rocks down to the sea, where they say the smugglers brought in their goods. It'll be fine, I'm sure, if you go slowly. I'll wait for you here with Colin. If you get into any difficulty, just yell.'

Holding onto a loose root, Bram stooped down, took a deep breath, glanced anxiously at the other two and carefully put one foot inside the hole to find the first step. The other foot in, then one further down for the next step and, after a short while and with a bit of manoeuvring, he edged his body through the opening to find that the ancient staircase, though narrow, could accommodate him with a little room to spare. The torch went on and his cautious footsteps slowly faded as he was lost from view.

'So do we just wait here?' asked Colin, as they watched the black hole.

'I suppose so,' replied Bob. 'The batteries in the torch I gave him are old, as I was asked, so it'll be dim for him down there but there's enough light from the gap down to the sea. And I threw Joe's bones in there too when I went in yesterday. I had a look around and it's safe if he's careful. No idea what he's looking for – it's just a damp old cave now. I don't think he'll stay long.'

They listened at the hole for a few minutes but all was silent. While they were waiting, Colin took the opportunity to tell Bob about his encounter up at the farm the previous evening, the voices behind the closed door, overheard possible plots and plans. Bob was intrigued.

'I think it might be the person, or people, who've asked us to help out with this,' Colin enthused, pointing at the hole. 'I mean, we know the person always does this sort of thing, gets others to help. I heard them mention Porlock, something about doing it for the village, whatever it is. It must be them!'

'You may be right,' Bob said, becoming interested. 'Did you hear anything else?'

'Not much,' admitted Colin, 'although I think I recognised one of the voices. I wasn't sure at first but I'm certain now'

'Oh yes?' prompted Bob.

'One of them was Raymond. And it makes sense. I mean, he's a farmer who's lived here all his life and everyone knows that the farming community here always tries to help out others in the area as best they can. Look at Vic's triathlon, for example. Maybe Raymond just likes to stay anonymous in case what he asks people to do turns out badly. So he won't get the blame.'

'That does sound possible,' Bob said thoughtfully. 'We all know Raymond, though, and I'm sure we'd know about it if it was him. And don't forget, you said he was talking to someone else, someone who may be involved as well.'

'Yes', replied Colin, 'There were two of them. I suppose it would need two to think up some of the things they ask us to do. Some of their ideas are quite elaborate.'

'They are,' said Bob. 'But I think it's best if we don't say anything about this to anybody. We may be wrong after all and, if Raymond is involved, he'll want to stay anonymous and we must respect that. Everything that's done has always turned out well and so we can't be the ones to spoil that.'

While they continued to wait, Bram was deep in the earth beneath them. The steps, old, worn and slippery from damp, seemed to be interminable, enclosed by a low stairwell roughly hacked from the rock no doubt several centuries ago. The daylight from above had faded completely by the time he reached the first turn. He slipped in the shadowy confines once or twice but pressed himself against the damp sides to steady his descent and his nerve. The dim beam from the torch illuminated no more than blackness ahead and only the faint sound of rushing encouraged Bram on in his growing fear that he was entering his own tomb. Doubts about the wisdom of this and the trustworthiness of the men above crowded his mind but, just as he was on the verge of going back, he turned another corner and saw faint daylight ahead.

Several more tentative steps down and the sides of the passage suddenly disappeared as Bram stepped into a huge empty space. From the far side at floor level, a small amount of daylight appeared, through which could be heard the gentle surging of waves on rocks and, to his left, a trickle of water splashed to the floor from a crevice above. He swung his failing torch around to see a large cavern filled with loose boulders of all sizes, seaweeded and slippery, cracked walls covered in slime, roots reaching through gaps, driftwood scattered around, impenetrable shadows in recesses, the musty smell of sea-washed age.

Still unnerved, he paused to take stock. The cave didn't seem in imminent danger of collapse and there seemed to be two exits – the stairs and an opening to the sea, where the smugglers must have gained access. He took a deep breath and remembered his purpose for being here – the Donna Maria and the hidden gold. With not much time available, he had to find out quickly if there was any evidence of recent activity, hidden corners, disturbed areas of rocks that might conceal a cache. If there was, he'd come back another time on his own, with tools if necessary.

He started on the back walls, peering up and down, around every jutting rock, into every ancient chasm and fissure. The torch was becoming ever dimmer but Bram's eyes had adjusted to the gloom and he was sure he could easily find his way back to the stairs. He continued to search, moving around one edge slowly, towards the gap to the sea. On the slippery floor he could now see outlines of more driftwood, natural wood as well as remnants of pallets, planks, possibly crates, that gave him a jolt of hope. And, among them, lots of smaller white shapes that looked out of place. He peered more closely and picked one up. A bone, fresh and white, cleanly cut through, traces of flesh still attached, a part of an arm or a leg, hopefully from an animal. In disgust, Bram dropped it to see, all around him, dozens more, scattered everywhere and concentrated more towards the gap.

His torch flickered weakly and then gave out completely and so he walked slowly towards the gap, eyes to the ground, trying to avoid the deathly scatter. The light was still dim, obscured by a large pillar of rock that filled much of the access to the sea. Bram moved carefully towards the hole, loose rocks everywhere, hoping to see how to get down to the sea, when he slipped. Cursing, he landed on his side, dropping the torch which bounced once and then briefly sprang back to life. Starting to raise himself, he glanced at the illuminated pillar in front of him and immediately cowered back in mortal dread. There, no more than a few feet away, was the devil.

Towering above was a large bulbous head stooping down towards him, glistening red eyes, long teeth, horns and scaly skin, and it was moving. He could feel his panic rising, alone and trapped in this cave whose walls seemed to be moving closer to him. He scrabbled backwards over the loose rocks and the figure above him moved again, leaning further towards him with a deep roar. All of a sudden, the roar turned into a cacophony of rumbles that filled the chamber and Bram found himself falling downwards as the ground beneath him gave way, sending him, a massive pile of rocks and the devil cascading down a slippery stone slope into the open air and the sea below.

Out in the bay, Pablo was on the deck of the Porlock Maria when he heard a sound like an earthquake. He turned and saw, at the foot of the cliffs not far away, what appeared to be a wall of rocks crashing into the sea, the water churning as stones and debris plummeted into the swell. But then...no, it's not possible...the head of a large sea serpent or dragon with horns emerged from the sea, its limbs flailing wildly in the turbulent waves. Remembering the local boys' story of the fierce creature that destroyed ships, he panicked.

'Oh, Dios mio, es un monstruo!' he yelled, loudly enough to attract other crew members below. Most were occupied elsewhere and only Fabio, young and reckless, heard the call. As he clambered up onto deck, Pablo had already loaded the first cannon and took out his box of matches. Frantically pointing to the writhing creature in the bay, he told Fabio to take the next cannon along. As Fabio started to load, Pablo put his lighted match to the fuse and, with a mighty boom, sent a plastic buoy hurtling towards its target. It hit the cliffs above the commotion, sending a shower of rock splinters splattering into the sea where the monster was still thrashing about. No more than 20 seconds later, Fabio fired his cannon, its load hitting the sea only 20 feet short.

By the time the rest of the crew, the recruits and the captain had come up on deck, two more shots had been fired. Seb yelled at Pablo and Fabio to stop and demanded an explanation. A huge and frightening sea creature with horns and big teeth, they said, that would surely attack them and sink the ship. Everyone looked towards the cliffs to see that the waves were as normal and that no monster, only what appeared to be a large wooden pole bobbing close to the shore, could be seen. They watched for a while further but, as the fun seemed to be over, Seb chastised the boys and sent everyone back to work.

Recovering behind a large boulder just above the tide-line was Bram. A few cuts and bruises from the fall and soaked to the skin from his immersion, he'd luckily avoided being knocked unconscious or worse by the rocks. He'd been tumbled into the sea and had grabbed a thick wooden pole that was in the water next to him before the ship had inexplicably started firing at him. He abandoned the pole, somehow scrambled to shore and took shelter behind the largest boulder he could find. As he sat there hidden, he saw the large pole in the waves close to him – an old pole with one end shaped and crudely painted as a dragon with only one horn remaining.

Cold, shaken and sore, he waited until the ship in the bay had quietened and the tide had fallen another few feet, before making his aching and weary way along the sheer coast and eventually back to the beach and safety.

13

It was as if a rose garden had stepped ashore. In a figure-hugging red top embroidered with thin intertwined green stems cascading down to thick ruffles of red and white roses, Elisa was eye-catching as she stood on the jetty and checked her bunned hair. By her side, Ramon, himself resplendent and elegant in black trousers, boots, hat and red silk shirt, allowed his sister to take his arm as they walked along the quay to the pub. Tonight at the Bottom Ship was Spanish Night.

The rest of the crew had already been in the pub for some time to help set up the evening, leaving just two to guard the ship. Cass was in the kitchen preparing the tapas, bo'sun José was decorating the dance floor and tuning his guitar, and the others were helping to clear the space, prime the staff and chat to inquisitive passers-by. Crates of Spanish cerveza and sangria had been provided by Ramon, whose idea this had been a couple of days previously. The simple posters had been plastered around the area at short notice – 'Spanish Night at the Bottom Ship, starts 7pm on Thursday 26 Sept. Spanish tapas and drinks available. Bring your dancing shoes! £5 entry, all proceeds to local charities.' Word had spread and they were expecting a good turn-out.

By the time Ramon and Elisa reached the pub, everything was ready. They made their way through the excitable queue that was already growing at the front and made their way to the back door to be let in by José. Inside, it looked fantastic – the tables had been rearranged around the dance area, colourful lights were looping across the walls, vibrant posters of flamenco stars had been hung, and the staff and Spanish assistants were all in flamboyant costumes. Elisa checked that Cass was on track in the kitchen and, final preparations done, background music on, smiles and thumbs up from all, they opened the door.

Within 20 minutes, it was standing room only. Tickets bought, many took the proferred glass of sangria and moved to the benches outside to enjoy the mild evening and the substantial plates of tapas that were served shortly afterwards. Everyone was in good humour, eager to enjoy this unusual social event in a week that had been full of surprises. Kat was there with Mark and his family, as were Pete and Eve and many of their friends, all enjoying the company of their new Spanish friends, and many others from the locality.

At 8pm, food finished and sangria still filling glasses, José strolled to his corner chair, picked up his acoustic guitar and started to play a short classical tune as the crowd slowly started to settle at the tables and benches around the room, those from outside standing wherever space allowed. When he'd finished, rowdy applause and cheering encouraged him to take a deep bow before he settled down again to wait for his cue. The coloured lights went on and, moments later, the side door opened to Ramon and Elisa who stepped majestically into the room and took their positions. José started up again, this time with a faster number as Ramon and Elisa began their dance – a flashing red swirl of stomping, sweeping, twirls and swoops, an exhilarating and emotional performance that left everyone, dancers and audience, breathless.

The crowd went wild. Smiles and thanks over, Ramon and Elisa were joined by four others of the Spanish crew who launched into a complex rhythmic piece that captivated the onlookers. A couple more dances followed and then, once the sangria and cerveza had loosened inhibitions, everyone was invited to join in. For the next hour, the floor resounded with a whirling melee of enthusiasm, some enjoying the expert guidance of the Spaniards and some couples going solo, until it was time for a breather.

Elisa and Ramon had been particularly in demand and so they headed straight to the bar for beers. Pete, Eve and Seb, sitting at a nearby table, squashed up to make room for them and, almost instantly, Ramon was surrounded by several fluttering ladies all eager for the next dance and to learn more about this intriguing and attractive man. Bombarded with questions, Ramon fended off the assault with ease, telling the ladies about his family's strong connection to Porlock, his desire to honour his grandparents' promise to provide a ship and his growing love for the place and its people over the last week.

'So, are you going to stay for longer?' twittered one of the ladies in hope.

'I am here for one week longer,' Ramon replied, 'and then, with great sadness, I must return home. My business calls me back.'

'And back to your wife?' asked another, pushing as close to him as she could.

'Yes, I am married,' he said. 'But ladies, if my situation changes, I will return here, I promise.'

While Ramon patiently chatted further to the giggling gaggle, Elisa had sat down next to Pete, downed most of a pint in one, and taken off her shoes.

'I needed that,' she said with a sigh, 'and my feet hurt. I need to rest.'

'You were great out there,' replied Pete as the others nodded in agreement. 'I would have joined in but dancing's not my forte, I'm afraid.'

'Nonsense,' chided Elisa, looking him in the eye. 'Everyone can dance, with the right partner and perhaps a bit of beer inside them. When we start again, you will dance with me.'

Despite protests, Pete allowed himself to be persuaded, secretly happy for the opportunity. With the arrival of Elisa at the table, it was no surprise that Pete became distracted, almost absorbed, by the Spanish beauty. Similarly, Eve seemed enchanted with Seb who had only joined in with two of the dances before collapsing, wheezing, at the nearest table. Not far apart in age, they had started chatting and discovered a common love for travel and adventure.

'Pete's father had Spanish ancestry, you know,' Eve told Seb, shuffling closer to him. 'And when he was younger, Pete travelled all around the seas there, to Spain, Italy, and Greece, didn't you, Pete?'

'I did,' Pete admitted. 'I loved it there, the way of life, the people, the food, everything. I've always felt drawn to Spain. Must be in my blood, I suppose.'

'Is a beautiful country,' said Seb gruffly in his thick accent. 'England is nice but Espana is the best. I like the drink and the food best, as you can see. But the women in Spain, they are very pretty but they shout too much. I think I like English women better.'

Eve tittered while Elisa frowned. 'Except Elisa,' Seb blustered, 'who is very beautiful and also very kind. And she is good boss too.'

The merriment continued and Pete went to the bar for more drinks. When he returned and handed another beer to Elisa, Eve noticed her gold ring that Pete was now wearing.

'I see you're wearing that old thing, son,' she said. 'I hope it brings you luck. Rik gave it to me, God rest his soul.'

'Did he ever tell you where he got it?' asked Pete.

'He said he found it in that old smugglers' cave along the coast a long time ago. It was probably from some old shipwreck – there's loads of them in these parts.'

'I asked an antiques expert about it,' Pete replied, 'and he said it might be a very old love token from South America, maybe even Inca, that's meant to bind lovers together forever. I checked online and he was right – a powerful and ancient love charm. To be honest, it sounds unlikely but then I'm just a cynic.'

'Oh, don't be so dull, Pete,' rebuked Elisa. 'To me, that sounds so romantic. It would be wonderful if the old magic really does work. I say you keep wearing it and see what happens.'

'But it isn't even mine,' Pete replied defensively, 'it's Mum's.'

'Oh, you can have it, Pete,' Eve smiled. 'It's no good to me now. It meant something to me once, when Rik and I were sweethearts and that ring bound us together. We even talked about getting married but...things didn't quite work out.'

'Why was that, Mum?'

'Well, your Dad came along in his flash Caddy and bowled me over. I was quite flighty back then.'

When the dancing continued later, Pete was true to his word and enjoyed an energetic and entertaining spin around the dancefloor with Elisa, to the envy of many onlookers. By this time, the revellers were warmed up and, without exception, everyone had a go. Seb led Eve sedately around the floor, showing her the slower flamenco moves whilst weaving between others, the Spanish youngsters spread their favours as best they could, Ramon was continually in demand, and Cass, when she emerged from the kitchen, flung herself into the fray with abandon. Even the older boys, who normally preferred to just prop up the bar, were persuaded.

The long evening eventually started to wind down as, tired and happy, the party-goers began to meander home. At their table, Eve and Seb had been talking and laughing non-stop, Pete and Elisa were enjoying each other's company and having an occasional dance, and Cass and Kat had perched at one end, chatting about their mutual passion for the food business and becoming good friends. The coloured lights were turned off, José packed away his guitar, nursing sore fingers, and the staff started to clear and tidy.

Pete and Elisa went outside and sat on the harbour wall, watching the clear night sky and the ship out in the bay, relishing the cool breeze, solitude and quiet murmur of the waves lapping gently on the quay. They sat in silence until Pete noticed Elisa glancing down at his gold ring.

'Your story about the ring,' she said quietly, 'it could be true. I think we all need a token of love, to give us hope and maybe some luck.'

'The Incas believed in it,' Pete replied, 'so maybe there is, or was, something in the legend. I believe that, if you're looking for love, you will eventually find it, with or without love charms. Some are happy to go through life without it, without all the problems it can cause.'

'Like you?' she asked. 'You are on your own and have never been married. Are you not lonely sometimes?

'Sometimes, yes,' he admitted. 'I've had relationships over the years but have decided to stay a confirmed bachelor. Love's a complicated and dangerous game. I'm happy as I am, carefree and single.'

'That sounds very sad,' said Elisa, taking Pete's hand. 'I think you want to find love but are afraid to. Maybe like me.'

Pete turned to her in surprise. 'You're an enchanting and beautiful woman,' he said. 'I'm sure you could easily find love if you wanted to.'

'That is the problem,' she said. 'All the men always want me just because I am pretty, they say. But in Spain, most men want their woman just to look after them and have babies. I am not like that. I like being myself. Ramon says I'm difficult.'

'He may be right,' Pete chuckled. 'My mother says the same about me – too independent and restless.'

'But you have lived here all your life, in this small place. Do you not want to have more adventures?'

'It would be lovely to,' he replied, 'but time's not on my side. I'm 56 and still have my mother to look after. She lives with me and depends on me. And I like Porlock and its people. On the other hand, I'd still like to travel while I can, explore the world more.'

'You're still young enough to have more fun, Pedro,' Elisa encouraged. 'I always try to have fun and I am not young anymore.'

'If only it was that easy,' he said, squeezing her hand. 'Maybe one day.'

She gave him a small kiss on the cheek. 'I like you and I think you will have more adventures if you want them. I say what I want and do what I want and you must do the same. Life is too short to sit inside and hope. Otherwise you will just get fat and die.'

He gave her a small kiss back, smiling. 'I like you too. If anyone can tame me, you can.'

'I do not want to tame you,' she fired back, 'I want you to be yourself. And you must wear that ring of your mother's all the time and we will see what happens then.'

Pete looked at her uncertainly. 'You mean, to see if the old spell might work?'

'Exactly! Who knows, the ring might be trying to bring us together. It will be fun to see if it really is magic.'

Pete looked her in the eyes and, despite his usual reticence, felt a strange and strong attraction towards her.

The moonlit stillness was interrupted by a gentle call from behind them and, turning, they saw Eve approaching.

'There you are, Pete,' she said. 'I've been looking for you. The pub's closing soon. It's time to go home, I think.'

Pete and Elisa looked back at each other with coy smiles.

'Yes, Mum,' Pete said, turning back towards Eve. 'I suppose so.'

'I must be getting back too,' said Elisa with a small sigh. 'Ramon and the others will be wanting to go soon and there's only one boat.'

Rising, Pete gave Elisa another kiss on the cheek and she wandered slowly back towards the quietening pub, leaving Pete and Eve at the silvery waterside. They sat on the wall and together watched the yachts bobbing in the harbour, flapping flags and ropes occasionally breaking the quietness in the light breeze.

'She's a lovely girl,' Eve noted eventually with a twinkle in her eye. 'You seem to be getting along very well together.'

'Yes,' Pete admitted quietly. 'She is lovely. We seem to be very similar in many ways. She's independent, strong, knows her own mind and lives on her own terms. I like her, Mum, I really like her.'

'I did notice the similarities,' said Eve. 'You've always been independent, especially after your Dad died. But it's never too late for something new, that's what I say.'

'That's what I keep telling myself, Mum. But the older I get, the more difficult it seems. To find someone special, I mean. All the girls I like were paired off years ago so I've come to terms with being on my own. And now Elisa's come along, out of the blue, and I feel an instant attraction.'

'You've only known her a few days,' Eve replied, holding his hand. 'She is very attractive but get to know her properly first before jumping in with both feet. You've done that before and been hurt.'

'I know. But I'm not getting any younger and can't wait forever. As you once told me, we no longer have the luxury of unlimited time so, if something feels right, you have to go for it.'

'I know,' said Eve, 'and I still believe that, especially at my age. Have fun while you can, is what I say. You're never too old for new adventures and, maybe, new loves.'

Pete smiled down at his mother and squeezed her hand. 'Thanks Mum.'

'Now,' said Eve after a pause, releasing Pete's hand and giving him a quick kiss on the cheek. 'Go back and find Elisa and arrange to see her again. She's a lovely girl and I know she likes you too. I'll sit here a short while longer. The sea looks quite serene tonight.'

'Thanks Mum,' he said again, smiling and returning the kiss, before striding quickly back to the pub.

14

Thursday afternoon was the traditional time for leisurely outdoor pastimes, when those with time on their hands, which normally included only retirees, enjoyed whatever took their fancy that week. It was approaching the end of September and, the weather still very agreeable, a group of nine men were on the recreation ground to relive past glories in the cricket nets. Two shared bats, gloves and sets of pads, three tatty balls and four bags of snacks and beers.

Three men rested on a bench, enjoying the cheery yells from the playground, the smell of the freshly cut grass, the cooling summer sun and the gentle knocks from the nets. Colin and Bob had both had a go at batting and bowling while Fred, now approaching 80, was happy just to watch, have a beer and natter with his friends. Vince was currently swinging his bat randomly and, muttering oaths, missing most of the balls tossed leisurely down by bowler James, while others sat on the far bench awaiting their turn. All had played for the village team over the years, with varying degrees of success.

While away from the others, Colin and Bob briefly filled Fred in on the activity of the previous afternoon. In the distance, the familiar portly figure of Joe crossed the field with a greeting wave and a beer was opened in anticipation. As he arrived, Joe took the can with thanks and, after gossiping briefly about the previous evening at the Bottom Ship, sat down on the end of the bench.

'I'm on next,' Joe told everybody, 'after Vince has finished.' He started to strap on the pads that were lying on the ground.

Another shouted oath from the nets as Vince missed another ball which struck his midriff. Jocular taunts from the bench on the other side as James laughed and 'Shall I try an underarm next time, Vince?' More swearing.

'I don't think I'll be in there for long today,' Joe continued, watching. 'I'm still tired from last night's event.'

'I missed it, I'm sorry to say,' replied Colin. 'I heard it was fun. I don't dance much though.'

'It was a good night,' agreed Joe. 'Those Spanish know how to party and the food was good too. I don't dance either but last night I had to have a go. That Elisa tempted me up and I couldn't say no.'

'Pete was another one who couldn't say no to her,' joined in Fred. 'He stuck to her like a limpet most of the evening. Not his usual self, was he, Joe?'

'No, he wasn't. He was like a teenager. Mind you, she is very attractive and Pete can't help himself.'

'I wish I'd seen it,' Bob giggled. 'Never stops trying does Pete.'

'Here, Bob,' said Joe, leaning in and in hushed tones. 'Before I go in or someone comes over, tell me how it went yesterday.'

Bob related quickly and quietly how the stratagem had worked, how Bram had been successfully lured to the cave, had gone in and then strangely disappeared.

'We waited for ages,' Bob continued, 'until, after maybe 30 minutes, I went in to look for him, in case he'd had an accident. We heard the cannons firing again from the ship and thought they were just having fun again, but we wanted to check that Bram was okay, just in case. The cave was the same as when I put the bones in on Tuesday. But Bram wasn't there. I looked everywhere but he'd gone. The only way out was through the gap to the sea. I looked - but nothing. We assumed he'd made his own way back.'

'Very strange,' said Joe thoughtfully. 'Why would he do that?'

'Well, Colin knows,' replied Bob. 'You saw him this morning, didn't you, Colin?'

'Ah, yes, I did. I thought he might have slipped down to the beach and, as the tide was low, he'd have been able to get back to the Weir without too much difficulty.'

'Yes?' prompted Joe, eager to hear the story before they were interrupted.

'He did do that, he told me,' Colin continued. 'I bumped into him and he apologised for not letting us know earlier but he'd had a bit of an embarrassing mishap, he said. He said it was a very spooky place, lots of bones everywhere, and he was getting very nervous, especially as it was dark and the torch gave out. He then said he thought he saw the devil in there and panicked, slipped and tumbled down to the sea. He couldn't get back up so made his way home across the rocks.'

'Didn't you tell us that he was frightened of the devil?' asked Bob.

'That's what he told us in the pub,' replied Colin. 'And Vince made up a story about a local legend of the devil that lives in the cave too. No wonder Bram was nervous. He admitted that his fear probably just fuelled his imagination, that what he thought was the devil was just a big chunk of driftwood.'

'And did he mention anything about Coleridge?' Joe asked. 'That's why he went into the cave, so he said.'

'I did ask him. He said there was evidence of an old waterfall and, as it's close to where Kubla Khan was written, it's likely that Coleridge visited the cave too. He said he'll add it to his research findings.'

'But did he seem rattled by it at all?' asked Bob.

'A little, I think,' replied Colin. 'He said he had a few bruises but I think he's made of sterner stuff. He asked me again about the haunted glade that was in Fred's papers, that he'd like to see it. He said the new information is worth looking into, for an article he's planning, apparently. I didn't tell him where it was as I don't trust him but did say that he'll need permission as it's on private land.'

'We still can't trust him,' said Joe. 'We've been told he's trying to undermine the Porlock Maria project and he's still sniffing around. Let's all keep an eye on him. If we're asked to help with anything again, I'm up for it.'

As the others all confirmed their assistance too, they were interrupted by Vince, red-faced and out of breath, calling Joe over for his spell in the nets. Joe lumbered over, put on his gloves and took the bat as Vince joined the rest on the bench and delved into a bag for another beer.

***

That evening, as the sun started to set in a rose-tinted sky, as the birds twittered and skittered through the trees and hedges in their endless dances, two sat in a remote garden, cold beers on the table.

T: 'I got another note last night, from Fan, wanting an update on how it went in the cave.'

M: 'Not as well as we'd hoped. I put the figurehead in there and everyone else had done their bit too. The South African thought he saw the devil and fell down into the sea, with a few cuts and bruises, and got back to the Weir over the rocks. He seems shaken, from what I hear, but not scared off.'

T: 'That's a shame but we knew the plan wasn't fool-proof.'

M: 'Apparently, he put it all down to his imagination, in his fright. He may be lying, may have worked out that it was staged.'

T: 'If that's the case, he might know that we're onto him too. We'll have to be better next time. He's still a threat, to the Porlock Maria and everything.'

M: 'And he was looking in about the right place where the gold was supposed to have been brought ashore.'

T: 'He's been asking strange questions up on the moor as well, about where the money for the ship came from. We need something else to get rid of him.'

M: 'Plan B?'

T: 'It'll have to be. We need him out of the way as soon as possible so will have to make the arrangements quickly. We might need to ask for help from the others.'

M: 'They're all solid, the ones who helped with the cave. They can be trusted to help out again and keep their mouths shut.'

T: 'Okay, let's prepare the wood. More scare tactics that may or may not work. We need to ask Joe for more bones.'

M: 'Fred's note mentioned the prize in a haunted wood and the South African's been asking about it. So, if he's hunting for the gold, he still doesn't know it's gone.'

T: 'But he still might find out the secret and tell the world. So let's get the wood ready, send a note to John whose land it's on and ask him to come along with his dogs and a shotgun when the time's right.'

M: 'We need to do it as quickly as possible. Once Bram finds out where the wood is, he's likely to get up there pronto.'

T: 'If he goes there without John's permission, which is likely, he won't go during daytime as there are too many estate workers up there. If he goes tonight, we've lost our chance. Let's hope he's still recovering from his encounter with the devil and goes tomorrow or Saturday. If I was him, I'd choose Saturday when everyone will be at the triathlon.'

M: 'We'll send out the messages to Joe and John tonight, then, and hope the plan works.'

T: 'And we have to keep a close eye on him at all times so that when it seems he's heading for the wood, we can put the plan into action. Keep your mobile on you.'

M: 'I'm sure John will agree – he hates trespassers, especially when the pheasants are out.'

T: 'Tonight I'll send an update to Fan who'll agree to our idea, I'm sure. Let's hope the plan works.'

M: 'And if it doesn't?'

T: 'Then we're out of options. If the South African is still sniffing around, we might need another, more final, plan for him. Although that's a last resort, of course.'

M: 'I'm glad we haven't had to do that during our time but I'm sure it's been necessary a few times over the centuries.'

T: 'My father told me that, apart from the woodcutter, he'd heard about only one other instance, about 100 years ago. The body was buried in the marsh. It's still there, probably.'

M: 'I always thought the marsh was a spooky place, especially at night.'

T: 'It's lucky we haven't needed to do anything so drastic, so far. But we did make a pact and we have to keep it.'

M: 'If the secret's in serious danger of being exposed and Fan asks us, of course. I wish we knew who he, or she, was. It'd be so much easier if we talked face to face instead of all these notes. Quicker too when time is pressing, like now.'

T: 'You know that we can't know who Fan is. Security. The system's worked for centuries.'

M: 'I know. Sorry, I'm just getting frustrated. I thought all of this would be over by now, all the gold used, everyone happy and no questions asked. Then this bloke comes along who could ruin everything.'

They looked hard at each other, jaws set, both steely-eyed, both 100 per cent resolute.

15

By eleven o'clock on Saturday, all car parks were full. At Porlock Weir at one end of Porlock Bay, the location of one of the change-over points and also of the finish, the main parking area had been filling rapidly with cars, trailers, television vans, coaches and pick-ups since nine, and the overflow parking in adjacent fields was almost at capacity too. The roads leading to the harbour were parked up on both sides, leaving scarcely enough room for the horse boxes to squeeze through to their dedicated parking. At the village of Bossington, the start of the triathlon at the other end of the long bay, it wasn't much better.

Mark and Spike were dropped off by Kat shortly afterwards, the boys to walk to the registration point close to the shore, while Kat headed back down to the Weir to set up her cake stall. The training on the Porlock Maria had been suspended for the day, a welcome break from the intensive regime. Registration opened at midday and the event didn't start until two o'clock and so there was plenty of time to get their bearings, meet friends, warm up properly and absorb the festival atmosphere. In the fields on the edge of Bossington, marquees and gazebos had been erected, television crews were setting up, interviews were taking place, a barbecue was on the go somewhere, there was a long queue at the tea and coffee trailer, and the beer tent was about to open. The sun smiled across the crescent bay, a gentle westerly breeze fluttering the flags that stood like sentries above the merchandise stalls. As Mark and Spike entered the busyness of the set-up, they searched keenly for friendly faces and rival competitors, but a throng of unknown faces seemed to be everywhere. Eventually they spotted their friend Harry looking equally disorientated and went over to meet him.

Together they walked to view the start, the rocky beach covered by more gazebos, bunting, dozens of kayaks lined up, photographers, sight-seers, another bustling hive of activity. As midday approached, they returned to the field and found the registration tent where Vic, elegantly dashing in chinos and blazer, was giving another televised interview. The boys joined the queue, greeting the other triathletes, most of whom they knew, all enthused with excitable and nervous anticipation. Family members milled around in support and word quickly spread of the scale of the competition – just over 40 entrants and only three were reckoned to be in the running. They didn't include Mark, Spike or Harry.

'We shouldn't listen to what they're saying,' Spike encouraged Mark. 'We've got as good a chance as any of them.'

'I know,' replied Mark cheerfully. 'I think it's an open race. We've all been training hard and I know I've got one of the best horses, so I'll give it my best shot.'

'Even if none of us get a place,' said Harry, 'we still get £50 if we finish, which isn't too shabby. Just don't sink, fall off your horse or twist an ankle.'

'You're right,' smiled Mark. 'I could do with the two grand first prize, like all of us, but the fifty quid is good too. I'm looking forward to it – it'll be a laugh.'

The registration took longer than anticipated as the competitors were checked in, given their numbers, handed the safety instructions, fitted with life jackets, and signed waiver forms. The last to arrive were the four Spanish boys, Carlos, Pablo, Fabio and Teo, looking relaxed and joking happily among themselves and dressed casually in T-shirts and shorts.

Eventually, shortly after one o'clock, all had arrived and been registered. Less than an hour until the start and the tension was palpable. Warm-ups began in earnest away from the increasing crowds, the marshals began to take their positions, messages were sent to the change-over points, and the atmosphere changed subtly from festivity to focus. The competitors were taken aside for a full briefing. Everyone was fully aware of the potential dangers.

All along the pebble ridge from one end of the bay to the other, spectators were scattered. On the rugged beach, the competitors waited beside their allotted kayaks and performed last-minute warm-up exercises. The crowds were held back, photographers and marshals flitted and, at one minute to two, Vic took his position to one side and reached for his whistle and flag. A last check with the chief steward, all athletes poised and watching, and Vic raised his flag, put the whistle to his mouth and, in one swift movement, brought down the flag and blew. They were off.

A frantic scramble as all 42 grabbed their kayaks and paddles and raced down the rocky beach to the sea as the crowd cheered them on. A couple of fallers and a lost shoe but, within seconds, most of them had put to water and had started powering west. The gentle swell of the sea and light wind rocked the colourful cascade of kayaks that slowly started to string out as a few competitors powered energetically to the front of the field although most were bunched in a central mass. From the shore, spectators followed their progress directly towards Porlock Weir in the distance, calling out encouragement until the kayaks had moved too far away.

In the bay, safety boats were shadowing the competitors. By the time the lead kayaks approached Porlock Weir, there had been five capsizes that had righted themselves and no other mishaps. The order of the field had been changing constantly as muscles started to ache, the initially keen ones flagged quickly, the methodical gained ground and the underdogs rose, so that, when the first kayak beached itself, most of the others weren't far behind. The massed crowds cheered and yelled on their favourites as, one by one, they landed, scrambled out of the kayaks and ran to the field close by where their horses were saddled and waiting. The large figure of Mark could be seen towards the front of the main group, Spike and Harry slightly ahead, and the Spanish boys scattered throughout.

Anne and her team were on hand to ensure that the horses were calm and clearly separated, as the athletes gradually reached their steeds, donned helmets and body protectors, and mounted, assisted by their allocated grooms. A grab of the reins and a quick kick and the horses galloped off at speed across the field and disappeared into the woods. Within ten minutes, all competitors had completed the change-over.

In the woods, the horses pounded and laboured uphill and onto the course that had been cleared and roped off, safety marshals on every corner and difficult turn. Along the route, pheasants, rabbits, squirrels and deer scuttled and squawked away from the huge creatures that thundered past again and again. Mud flew in all directions, fallen twigs were trampled to splinters, low-hanging branches were avoided and clouds of hot breath filled the air as the horses galloped up and down the footpaths, deer trails and old tracks that weaved through the ancient and unkempt woodland. No spectators were permitted on this section and so the horses thumped on undisturbed and unimpeded, heading towards Porlock and eventually down the hillside towards the farm on the edge of the village. As the riders began to emerge from the woods, Callum, a farmhand on George's farm, was in the lead. The eager crowd watched as the rest of the riders came into the field at the next change-over point. Leaving the panting horses in the hands of the team of grooms there, the mud-splattered competitors removed their riding equipment and swiftly changed into their running shoes, and set off across country on the final section back towards Porlock Weir. Mark had gained a few places on the ride and was now in fourth place, his friends not far behind. Word quickly spread that there had been two fallers in the woods, one with a suspected broken ankle.

Down at Porlock Weir, the excitement and anticipation were growing. The marshals had been alerted that the runners were on their way, the crowds were moved back behind the ropes, mobiles were buzzing with updates, a brass band was warming up and the winning-line tape was being prepared. Everyone was jostling for a view along the home straight, the locals in the know having already moved to the best vantage points in the sloping fields above the hamlet, binoculars at the ready. Among them were Joe, Bob and Colin, the latter clicking liberally with his camera and long lens. They all chatted amiably to other friends there, discussing the event, the small wagers placed, the new sense of purpose in the village. Raymond was also close by, having given Jack a lift down with his costume for the small pantomime promotional show by the harbour and he was soon joined by Vic, who had arrived from Bossington and wanted a break from the endless interviews and attention for a short while. They both watched intently from the hillside, on the sidelines as usual.

'There's Jack,' said Vic, eyes pressed to his binoculars, 'in his Smee costume, waving his wooden sword about. What a sight! I hardly recognised him, with all that make-up and the fat suit. You'd never catch me doing that in a thousand years.'

'He enjoys it,' chuckled Raymond, eyes to binoculars too. 'And look, just over to the right. There's that South African, sunglasses and hat, on his own. Seems he survived the cave.'

'Yes, looks like he's bounced back,' replied Vic, turning his binoculars. 'Still looks shifty though. He's gone into the crowd now. Think I've lost him.'

They turned their attention to the other activities on this festival day – the barbecue, the Pantomime Society's performance, Morris dancers, stilt walkers, face-painting, ice-creams, bunting and balloons, a brass band, all contributing towards a relaxing and fun-filled afternoon. The first runners were expected to arrive in less than 30 minutes and so those in the field overlooking the old fishing port relaxed, opened a few beers, chatted and waited.

After a while, above the general noise of crowds, music and excitement down below, they could hear distant shouting and, turning towards its source, by the old row of thatched cottages that faced onto the beach, they saw several agitated people together, arms waving, some shouting, one clearly upset. Raymond and Vic, too far away to hear any details, watched the scene through their binoculars and saw someone stride away and summon the two policemen that had been meandering casually through the crowds. The police arrived with the group and, after a brief discussion, everyone went around the back of the cottages and out of sight.

'Seems there's been an incident of some kind,' observed Raymond.

'I have to go down there shortly,' said Vic, a worried look on his face, 'for the presentations. I don't want anything to mar the day. I'll find out what I can and let you know.'

They both scanned the crowds for any other clue but noticed nothing unusual.

Bram, they saw, had reappeared near the harbour, a distance from the cottages but watching the activity there with apparent interest.

Meanwhile, on the hillside, Joe, Colin and Bob had an opportunity to break away from their group of friends for a brief catch-up, before the runners arrived. Well out of hearing of anybody else, Joe told Colin and Bob about an additional request he'd received on Thursday night, to help out with the 'South African problem' once again, although he'd been asked not to discuss the details with anybody else.

'So all that stuff with the cave didn't work,' said Bob, 'as we guessed. I know you can't tell us anything about it, Joe, but I hope it works this time, whatever it is. I haven't been asked to do anything else.'

'Nor me,' said Colin.

'I can't tell you anything, as you know,' replied Joe. 'I know only what I've been told to do, nothing else. It's still a mystery to me.'

'Well,' Colin said tentatively, keeping his voice low. 'I might have a small clue about what's going on. Bob knows and we agreed that we'd let you know too, Joe. We can trust you and you may be able to help as well.'

As quickly as he could, Colin filled Joe in on the chance encounter up at Vic's farm, of the strange overheard mutterings behind closed doors, a secret discussion about the future of Porlock, of Raymond's involvement.

'Bob and I have had a chat,' Colin went on, 'and, the more we think about it, the more obvious it seems. I mean, the farmers have always helped out the community and, if they know that Bram is causing problems with the Porlock Maria venture, they'd be the first to offer help. I heard all this at Vic's farm so it's likely that Vic is involved, with Raymond and maybe others.'

'So,' Joe said, musing, 'that means that they're probably in league with the Spanish, that Ramon bloke, who gave the ship to Porlock.'

'Sounds probable,' Bob said. 'Although, if there are so many people involved and the South African is still causing problems, surely they must be able to shut him up somehow themselves. Why involve us and why all the secrecy?'

'No idea,' replied Joe. 'But, tell you what, I'm up delivering at Vic's farm on Monday so I'll ask around, see if I can find out anything.'

Below them, a few shouts could be heard that slowly spread to a general cheer as the first of the runners came into view, entering the last of the fields several hundred metres away. Not far behind, two others were neck-and-neck and, way behind, a few others grouped together. Bob raised his binoculars.

'Looks like Amy's in the lead. Amy Watson,' he said as he continued to scan.

'Good for her,' replied Joe. 'I see her out running most days and she's got her young family, struggling on benefits, I hear. If she wins, I'm really happy for her.'

'What about the next two?' asked Colin.

'Tim Farley and Tom Hudson, I think,' said Bob. 'Both in the running club. I can't see who's leading the pack behind them but, looking at the size of one of them, it could be Mark at the front.'

The runners came off the field and onto the short road section towards the finish as the vast crowds cheered them home. Amy hit the winning line at a good pace to rapturous applause and cheers. Tom just managed to ease ahead of Tim into second place and, behind them, Callum took fourth and the surprisingly brisk Mark came fifth. The following straggling group contained Spike and Harry, puffing like steam trains and, towards the back, most of the Spanish boys together, reduced almost to a walk. Still cheerful and playing to the crowds, they gladly accepted congratulatory kisses from eager young admirers.

Vic had gone down to the winning line in time for the finish. While the crowds eagerly waited for the last runners to arrive, he'd had a quick word with the policemen, now joined by two colleagues who had parked discreetly up the road.

Once Vic had the full story, he called Raymond who was still on the hillside.

'Seems one of the cottages has been broken into,' Vic explained. 'Molly's, the one next to Kat's house. A back window was smashed and they got in there. Nothing was taken apparently, just lots of mess – furniture moved, drawers opened, a bit of damage but nothing serious. Must have happened while everyone was distracted by the event. Molly's very shaken.'

'Any clue who did it?' asked Raymond.

'The police are asking around,' Vic replied, 'but they've drawn a blank so far. They'll be here for a while, taking statements. I've asked them to keep a low profile so it doesn't spoil the day.'

'That Bram was loitering near there.'

'Raymond, it could have been anybody. There's hundreds of people here, most of them from out of the area. It could have been any chancer.'

'You're right,' replied Raymond with a sigh. 'Let's hope the police find the culprit soon.'

'I'll keep you updated,' said Vic. 'I've got to go now. More duties to perform. Catch you later.'

The festival continued for all of the afternoon. Once the speeches, prize-giving and presentations were over, the Porlock Maria fired an eight-gun celebratory salute and the party began in earnest. The competitors enjoyed their free pint, a rock band replaced the brass band, the food stalls and barbecue coped with the demand, the television crews packed up and joined in, sunbathers and swimmers enjoyed the afternoon sun and José led some impromptu Spanish dancing. It was a joyous afternoon that spilled into the early evening.

On a bench by the shore, Bob, Colin and Joe had come down from the hill and were enjoying another leisurely pint as the sun started to dip. The police had gone, the crowds had begun to disperse, the day-trippers heading home, allowing die-hard locals to gather and chat at their own pace. Familiar faces from all through the Vale were there, prolonging what had been a successful and entertaining day for the area. The ship glistened in the bay although most of the crew were on shore and still celebrating in earnest.

Bob picked up his binoculars to scan the crowds and saw John, Jack, George and Raymond at a table with beers, a bottle of whisky next to John, the winner of the sweepstake. Ramon, Elisa, Pete and some of the ship's crew were laughing together on an adjacent table.

At a distance away, by the harbour wall, stood Bram, tall and solitary in his Panama hat and sunglasses, watching everything, motionless.

16

It was early evening on the following day when Joe got the call. He was in the Bottom Ship enjoying a beer with Sam the baker, a fellow trader, where all conversations still centred around the triathlon of the previous day. There were already rumours that other local alternative triathlons were being planned for others in the area, to complement the main event next year and to raise more funds for the local young. One idea of pool, darts and skittles competition, to be known as the Pubathon, was gaining traction and members of the Porlock Retirees Club, known affectionately as the Porkers, were planning a similar event with tennis, bowls and croquet. It would be called the Porkathon.

Joe put down his phone, downed his pint, made his excuses to Sam and headed for his car. The call had come from John, with the message that the South African had been reported leaving the village and heading up the moor towards the wood. All eyes had been on Bram to check when he would make his move and it appeared that this was the time.

Joe took the back roads that led to the edge of the wood and parked up quietly in the shadows of the firs. All quiet, nobody about, no other vehicles. A pheasant called from close by and a single startled blackbird chirruped and flapped into the undergrowth. He quickly hauled the stinking sack from the back of his car, went through a gate and made for the open glade in the wood.

The rough path jagged tightly through the ancient and twisted woodland, moss-covered trees slowly turning ghostly silver as the sun started to dip and the shadows lengthened. Soon enough, he reached the circular clearance, the hint of low standing stones around the perimeter, reaching out of the decaying ferns like timeworn teeth. He stopped and looked around carefully. At his feet, the early evening mist was starting to rise, light swirling wisps slowly creeping over the damp ground. An uneasy silence had descended as if time was holding its breath. All birdsong had ceased. This place always gave Joe the jitters, especially at twilight. Standing there in the open, he felt an unusual nervousness as if countless soulless eyes were peering at him from deep recesses. The spectral reputation of the wood was well deserved. Chiding himself for a fool, he took a deep breath and got to work, spreading the rotting bones around. All done and keeping one cautious eye over his shoulder, he quickly retreated into the dense darkness of the thick tangle of low branches. He sat down and waited.

In the eerie stillness, he didn't have to wait long. The ruffle of pigeons taking flight nearby heralded the arrival of something and, sure enough, a tall dark figure could be seen weaving slowly through the trees towards the glade. It was unmistakably the South African and he was holding a long thin case. At the edge of the opening, Bram stopped and looked around uncertainly, sniffing the damp air. He stood a few tentative steps into the open, glancing at the ground, and suddenly paused, staring downwards. Bones, lots of them, fresh, some with meat still attached, scattered everywhere. Bram looked up and around the area, peering nervously into the dark edges for signs of life, of possible danger.

Joe shrank lower and held his breath. Total silence.

A few static moments passed as Bram appeared to reconsider. And then he seemed to gather himself and slowly unzipped the case, withdrawing an implement of sorts. He pressed a button which was followed by a quiet beep. A metal detector, Joe could now see. Leaving the case to one side, Bram immediately started scanning the ground methodically, sweeping the detector back and forth while walking cautiously from one side of the glade to the other. Every few steps he stopped, looked around, listened, and then resumed. He reached a standing stone, turned and walked back the other way, pausing occasionally. No signals yet.

He continued in this way for several minutes as Joe silently watched from the deepening shadows. The swirling mist was becoming denser and the temperature was dropping. The only sound was the soft crunching of Bram's feet across the ground. Light rustles in the undergrowth, spiders silently spinning, imagined whispers, tension in the growing gloom.

Bram seemed to sense the change too. After a couple of sweeps up and down, and with nothing to show for it, he paused and again looked around. The absolute silence was broken by a few pigeons flapping overhead and, shortly afterwards, another flock took flight noisily, this time much closer. As he stood motionless in the gloom to check if anything was approaching, the silence was shattered by an enormous explosion – a shotgun blast, no more than 30 yards away, followed immediately by the barking of large dogs. Bram, in a panic, dropped to his knees and tried to hide behind a thick gorse bush but it was too late.

Two dark dogs, Huntaways, came charging into the clearing, yapping, noses to the ground. In a flash, they eagerly grabbed a bone each before one of them turned and saw Bram. It stopped, dropped the bone, snarling, teeth bared, hackles up. The second dog noticed and turned towards Bram too. A moment later, their owner lumbered out of the wood, shotgun in hand.

'Sally, Shadow, stay!' he shouted as he saw the man cowering in fright in front of them.

The dogs did as they were bidden, quiet now but eyes still firmly fixed on the stranger in case their master changed his mind.

'Who are you and what the hell are you doing on my land?' he shouted, shotgun loaded and still held tightly in both hands.

'I…I'm sorry,' blustered Bram as he started to get to his feet. 'I didn't know this was private land.'

'Of course it is! Didn't you see the signs? You've no right to be here! And what's that you've got with you?'

'I thought I'd try a bit of metal detecting, just for the fun of it,' he stumbled, standing up. 'It's my hobby. I didn't think it would be a problem.'

'Of course it's a problem,' returned the man loudly. 'Not only is this private land but this is a scheduled monument too. I should call the police.'

Bram looked worried. 'No need for that,' he replied, now starting to gather himself and standing firm. 'I just thought it would be okay. If it's a problem, I'm sure we can come to some arrangement.'

'The only problem is you,' retorted the man. 'I don't like trespassers and I don't like you.'

He held his shotgun more closely as the dogs, sensing their master's anger, poised themselves for the order. The man took a deep breath as Bram fearfully waited for his decision. He didn't have to wait for long.

'Just get off my land now!' he shouted at last, 'before I change my mind. If you're not gone in ten seconds, I swear I'll set my dogs on you and, when they're done, I'll give you a blast where the sun don't shine!'

Bram didn't need a second invitation. Turning, he trotted swiftly back down the faint path into the woods and back to his car. The distant sound of the car starting and then he sped away.

In the shadows of the wood, Joe watched and smiled before slowly emerging. John was admiring the metal detector that Bram had left behind and the dogs were happily gnawing on a couple of bones, glancing up at the familiar figure of Joe as he approached. John looked up and saw him.

'Was that all right?' John asked, smiling too.

'Oh yes, I think you did very well,' Joe replied.

'I was asked to scare him away and I think he looked scared enough to me.'

'I was scared too, you old sod. I'm just happy that the dogs know me.'

John chuckled. 'They wouldn't hurt you. They know they'd lose their best supplier of bones. I'll let them keep a couple and I'll leave the rest to the birds and foxes. You can have this metal detector, if you'd like it?'

'Thanks,' said Joe, taking it. 'I give it a go. You never know, I might find some gold.'

As the men started to leave, both dogs suddenly stopped gnawing and raised their heads in unison, as if they'd heard something. Hackles went up and, although the men strained to hear any unusual sound, all was silent.

'We need to leave here now,' said John a little nervously. 'I've lived on this land all my life but this wood still gives me the creeps. There's creatures in these woods that no man should meet, believe me.'

The dogs didn't need any prompting to go. As they all returned quickly to their vehicles, the darkness and deathly silence of the wood intensified, the mist thickened and the shadows reclaimed the glade.

17

He was rattled. Rattled and jumpy. He hadn't slept well after that episode in the woods last night, images of wild dogs, demons, stinking bones, burial alive, fingers on triggers, ghosts in the shadows, his life in the balance, all swirling wildly in his head. He thought South Africa was a dangerous place for the likes of him but these people here, on the surface so mild and friendly, had dark depths that he had underestimated. But…no, maybe not. He knew he was tired after a bad night and his imagination could be playing tricks. He needed to think it through with a clear head.

A late breakfast at the B&B, a couple of strong coffees and Bram found a sunny and tranquil spot in a corner of the immaculate garden. Hat and sunglasses on, he watched the distant sea and listened to the calming birdsong. He took the well-worn photocopy from his pocket and he studied it once again.

He'd been very lucky to have come across it. While researching Crusader treasures in a small provincial Spanish museum last year, he'd chanced across the document. He'd surreptitiously photographed it, just in case it proved lucrative. After many months of research, he'd pieced together an extraordinary tale, of battles, theft, gold and secrecy. It was possibly only a legend but, working on a hunch, he had decided to come to Porlock.

But now, after one week, he was less sure. On the one hand, he felt that he was being played, that the locals knew what he was up to, that they were trying to scare him off. On the other hand, nobody had challenged him directly and he was certain that they were trying to hide something. The substantial anonymous donations over the years and the arrival of the Porlock Maria were far too coincidental.

Bram could sense that he was on the right track and getting close but he had to work quickly. Time was against him and the net could be closing. A game of cat and mouse, and he wasn't going to be the mouse. Once he found the spoils, he'd need to escape immediately. He went back inside the B&B, checked the safe where his several passports were kept, made himself another coffee and planned his next move.

18

Like children, they jumped off the quayside into the cool water below, shouting as they went, much as they had done since they were youngsters together. Built with a bit more ballast these days, all three landed with impressive splashes and came up spluttering a few moments later, much to the surprise and amusement of the tourists wandering past. Joe and Colin sat on the harbour wall, legs dangling over the edge, and watched them.

'The old fools should know better by now,' observed Joe. 'Wouldn't catch me doing that.'

'There's no harm in it,' replied Colin cheerfully. 'Okay, Fred's well over 70 now but he still looks sprightly. In fact, he's got a better physique than Bill and Bob, I reckon, and they're much younger.'

'A trio of ancient walruses flapping about, that's what I think.'

'Oh. Don't be so miserable, Joe. It looks fun. I've half a mind to join them. It's a warm day and they say the weather's going to break soon so we may as well enjoy it while we can.'

They watched their friends enjoying themselves in the quiet harbour who were soon joined by three excitable young children released by their watchful parents. Out in the bay, the Porlock Maria was returning majestically to its anchorage having completed its first full training voyage up the coast and back again. The lunchtime sightseers meandered casually about as if time was endless and the benches outside the pub were slowly filling. Colin and Joe, friends for several decades, enjoyed the tranquil scene, contemplating the strange events of the last ten days that had caused sensation locally and nationally, and both wondered what all of it would bring to the village.

Before Joe returned to his shop after his lunch break, he updated Colin on the episode in the wood a couple of days ago. John played his part well, he said, and Bram was visibly shaken. Joe also reported that he'd visited the Williams' farm on his rounds yesterday and had had a quiet word with Vic about Raymond and their suspicions, and the promise of total confidentiality.

'Vic did tell me something,' Joe told Colin quietly, 'but I've been sworn to secrecy. I'm sorry but I can't tell you anything, at this moment anyway. You'd understand if you knew.'

Colin knew better than to probe further and so, after watching the bathers in the harbour and the ship settling in the bay for a few minutes longer, Joe headed back to his van. As he drove off, he saw Pete walking towards Kat's house and gave him a cheery wave, half-heartedly reciprocated.

Inside, Kat welcomed Pete with a warm hug. He didn't seem his normal jovial self and so Kat sat him down, put the kettle on and made small-talk as she prepared the teas.

'How's Molly?' Pete asked.

'She's okay, I think,' Kat replied. 'A bit shaken but she's getting better. Men are coming in today to fix the window and get more locks on the doors.'

'They still haven't found out who did it yet,' Pete went on. 'They guess it wasn't a local. Possibly just a kid looking for trinkets, an opportunist. At least nothing was taken. Must have been disturbed.'

'If I'd been at home at the time,' Kat said, filling the teapot, 'and found him there, he wouldn't have left in one piece.'

'I believe you,' smiled Pete. 'You're still fiery, Kat. Some people here are still afraid of you, even after all these years.'

'Yes, I know,' Kat said reflectively, sitting down and pouring the tea. 'But my hair is going grey and I am much calmer now. I struggled in Porlock at first. It has not been easy, the fire still burns sometimes but I am happy here now. If anybody threatens to upset this, I will fight back, I am sure of it.'

Pete smiled back, took a sip of his tea and gazed out of the window. Kat nibbled a biscuit quietly as they both sat there in silence for a few moments.

'Noddy's been up in the woods much more at the moment,' Kat said in passing. 'He keeps coming back with fresh bones. I think a sheep must have died up there although some of the bones seem too big.'

'Oh yes?' mumbled Pete, somewhat distracted.

'I suppose it could be the annual culling of the tourists,' she joked, trying to raise a smile. 'I have heard a few shots up there recently and there are fewer day-trippers here today.'

'Yes, maybe,' Pete replied distractedly, picking up a biscuit.

Kat was about to pour more tea but instead put the pot down firmly on the table.

'Okay, Pete, what's up?' she demanded. 'Your face looks like a flapping flounder, as Will used to say. You've got something on your mind. Tell me. Is Eve okay? Are you okay? Or somebody we know?'

'Everyone's fine,' replied Pete quietly.

'So tell me, Pete, please. I haven't seen you like this, you are usually so happy. If everyone is okay, then...'

She paused and looked hard at him and he peered meekly up at her.

'Oh no, Pete,' she said, a smile starting to grow. 'I think I know what it is. I have seen you like this only once, maybe a few years ago. I think...I think that you are maybe getting very fond of someone?'

Pete glanced back at her coyly and sighed.

'I knew it!' Kat exclaimed. 'It is that Elisa, isn't it? The Spanish woman you have been spending so much time with. I thought I saw some signs but then said to myself, no, it is Pete just having his normal fun with the ladies. Oh, Pete.'

She took his hand and he gently squeezed hers.

'I don't know what it is about her,' Pete admitted. 'It feels like I am being drawn to her with every breath I take, even though I met her only about ten days ago. We've been spending a lot of time together, we have fun, she makes me smile and we seem like kindred spirits, whatever that is supposed to mean. I think she likes me too.'

'Of course she does,' Kat replied. 'Any fool can see that. You two are well suited.'

'It's caught me by surprise. I haven't felt like this for a very long time. I was planning just to carry on as I am, on my own and enjoying all the flirting. Although, lately, I have been thinking about settling down.'

Kat poured the tea. 'Life takes strange turns all the time,' she said. 'Go with the flow and listen to your heart.'

'I did think, just for a moment, that you and I would make a good couple, Kat. You know, we'd keep each other company and maybe laugh our way together into married old age.'

'Oh Pete,' she smiled. 'It's a lovely idea but very silly. I do love you but not like a lover. You're my best friend, why spoil that with marriage? Anyway, we'd drive each other mad. If your heart is drawn to Elisa, let your heart take you to her.'

'But what can I do? She's going back to Spain at the weekend.'

'Have a chat with her, tell her how you feel. It can't do any harm and you'll find out how she feels too. You never know, it may be good news.'

'I might, if I can find the time and the courage. Me and Mum have been invited on board this evening for drinks. I'll see how it goes. I think Mum and the captain, Seb, are getting along famously as well. They seem to like each other.'

'I'm glad,' smiled Kat. 'Find the courage and enjoy the evening. Tell me all about it tomorrow.'

She gave him a lucky kiss on the cheek as the front door opened and Mark stepped loudly into the room.

'I'm knackered,' he announced as he sat down heavily. 'We left at seven o'clock this morning, been up the Channel as far as Burnham and back, working really hard. Learning the ropes, literally. And I've got a fence to fix up on George's farm this afternoon as well.'

'Stay there,' said Kat, 'and I'll get you something to eat. There's still some tea in the pot if you'd like some.'

'I'd rather have a beer,' Mark replied, 'but I'd better not.'

'All this hard work will be worth it,' said Pete reassuringly as Kat went off to the kitchen, 'especially if you get the job on the ship.'

'Oh, that reminds me,' said Mark. 'I forgot to say. Mum!' he shouted. 'Good news! They've offered me the job of Chief Carpenter.'

'That is brilliant news, Marco!' beamed Kat as she hastened back into the room carrying plates. 'I am so happy for you. Well done!' as she gave him a hug and a kiss.

'It's not full time as you know,' Mark replied. 'I'll be needed only occasionally when the ship's here, as it's new, but I'll be sailing with it when it goes off around the world. The pay's good and it'll be an adventure.'

'But what about Beth and Amy when you're away?' asked Pete.

'We've talked about it,' said Mark. 'I'll still be working here when I'm home and the pay on the ship is better, so overall we'll have more money coming in. If things get tight, Beth can get a job in a shop or pub and Mum said she can look after Amy if I did get the job.'

'That's right,' Kat replied. 'We'll sort it out somehow.'

'I don't want to leave Beth, Amy and you, Mum, for all that time but I think it's a good opportunity that could lead to other things. And I'd do anything to get in extra money at the moment.'

'I heard about your problems with the landlord, Mark,' said Pete. 'If there's anything I can do, just ask.'

'Thanks, Pete. We'll get by somehow and the job on the ship will help enormously. I was hoping to do better in the triathlon but I won £50 which helps a bit, of course.'

'You never know, Mark,' Kat chipped in. 'That new development in the village – they might decide to build some affordable starter homes after all, which will help.'

'Fat chance, Mum,' Mark replied despondently. 'They'll be just big expensive houses for retired people or more blooming second homes.'

'I'm here anyway,' replied Pete, 'for advice or any other help you need. Things are changing quickly around here at the moment and for the better. Stay optimistic, Mark – you're doing well and I'm sure it'll all work out somehow.'

***

On board that evening, Pete and Elisa were leaning on the deck railing of the Porlock Maria, rocking gently in the sway of the bay, glasses in hand, watching the lights of the Weir. The barrel of beer, donated by Vic for the Spanish crew after the triathlon, was almost empty and so Ramon had acquired another one for the crew who were lounging elsewhere on deck and below after a long day. Eve was below decks somewhere with Seb, Ramon was on shore, and Cass made the occasional appearance with platters of warm tapas for the two guests. The deck was quiet and Pete and Elisa, side by side, were enjoying the solitude.

Pete was nervous. It was Tuesday, only nine days after he'd met Elisa, and she was due to go home on Sunday. They were talking pleasantries and Pete was finding it awkward. Having been purposefully distant in most of his recent brief relationships, he was unpractised in demonstrative displays of emotion. And yet he knew that, this time, something powerful had flicked a strong switch in his soul, something he was incapable of resisting despite his natural caution. Trapped in inner turmoil, his words were stumbled, mumbled, and he felt like a helpless and impotent child. Elisa noticed.

'What is wrong with you tonight, Pete?' she asked in concern. 'You are not yourself. You are usually so chatty and happy but tonight you are quiet. Do you not like me any more?'

'No,' said Pete, jolted out of his bluster and turning to look at her. 'That's not it at all, I promise. I just…I'm just thinking about the weekend.'

'Yes,' Elisa replied quietly. 'I have been thinking about that as well. I am here for only a few more days. I am not sure I want to go quite yet, Pete.'

She gazed out across the water to the twinkling lights on shore.

'I like it here. Your country is very beautiful, I like the people here very much and, Pete, I like you very much too.'

Pete, feeling his heart thumping, summoned his courage and took her hand. He could easily chat the chat when he wasn't serious, but this was very different.

'I like you very much as well, Elisa,' he replied breathlessly as they gazed at each other. 'I don't want you to go either. In fact, I would like to spend much more time with you. If that's okay with you.'

She smiled at him. 'That would be lovely, Pete. I would also love to see you more, to get to know you, the real you, more. I think we could have a lot of fun together and make each other very happy.'

Pete felt his nerves start to fade as she moved closer to him, still smiling.

'But what can we do about it?' he whispered tentatively.

'I'm sure we can think of something,' she said quietly before gently kissing him.

19

Thursday late afternoon; football practice on the recreation ground. The two old friends sat on the last empty bench, ice creams in their hands, and watched the youngsters going through their paces. It was still warm yet dirty clouds were flitting in from the west and the air was cooling. The long hot summer was almost over.

It was a good time and place to chat, to re-evaluate.

M: 'Here we are, among all these people, and nobody knows who we are. I mean, they know who we are but not WHO we are.'

T: 'You're right. They're not watching us, scarcely noticing us. We're invisible.'

M: 'Well, we are ghosts after all. Living another life, unseen by others.'

T: 'I know. It's been difficult living like this.'

M : 'I was hoping it would all be over by now.'

T: 'Me too.'

M: 'The plan worked. The ship has been a success, the gold is gone, the authorities are happy, everything is rosy. Except for one thing.'

T: 'The South African.'

M: 'Yes, him. And, to a lesser extent, the rumours I've heard, about Raymond.'

T: 'I've heard that too. There's talk that Raymond may be the one who's been sending out the anonymous requests for help.'

M: 'But only those involved have been talking about it and haven't told anybody else, I hope. I was thinking – is it possible that Raymond is Fan? I mean, we don't know who Fan is but someone like Raymond, from one of the old farming families, could easily be the one.'

T: 'It's possible. We don't know and, now that all this is almost over, we'll probably never know. I think it's best it stays like that.'

M: 'You're right, it should remain a secret forever.'

T: 'The rumours about Raymond will soon die down. But we still have a problem with the South African. He hasn't been scared away and he must know we're onto him. If he hasn't guessed the truth by now, it's just a matter of time 'til he does. We, and Fan, have a decision to make.'

M: 'I know.'

T: 'If Fan sends the instruction, we need to work quickly. And not make any mistakes.'

M: 'I'm ready, able and willing. By the way, did you bring your coin? It's probably the last time they'll be together in one place, after so many centuries.'

T: 'Yes, here it is. Souvenirs for us and the very last of the gold. I'll hide it away somewhere and try to forget everything, once it's over.'

M: 'Me too. Here's mine. It'll all be over soon, one way or another. It'll be lovely not having to worry anymore.'

T: 'Just one last thing to do.'

And with that, the two finished their ice creams and made a plan, down to the very last detail.

***

In the deepening shadows of the evening, Bram hid and waited. He'd finally worked it all out and it all now made sense. Porlock Weir was the centre of everything, the original wrecking, the Porlock Maria, the smuggling heritage, even the people he suspected might be trying to thwart him. He'd been watching the house of the widow and seen lots of suspicious activity – the ship's cook had been visiting on occasion, the widow's son was working on the ship, and that dandy Pete who was friends with the men who'd shown him the cave had visited often. It was obvious to him now - the gold was hidden in the widow's house, not the one next door. This could be his last chance to find it.

He'd done the planning the day before. Thursday night was the local women's group weekly social night up in Porlock Village Hall, 8pm start, and was usually just a get-together of sorts followed by a drink at the Top Ship. Tonight, the cook from the Porlork Maria was giving a talk and demonstration on Mediterranean cooking. The widow always attended and always with her big dog, he'd learnt,

112

who enjoyed the company of other canine friends in the pub. The house would be empty and there were no signs of an alarm.

He waited until 8.30pm. The Bottom Ship down the road seemed busy but there were only a few sitting outside. The house was quiet with just one internal light on, probably just a security light. Sensible, if there was something worth stealing there. He stepped out of the shadows, pulled up his face-mask, and walked unseen to the back of the house.

Inside the house, the glorious smells of warming meze dishes filled the small kitchen. Kat sat at the table with a glass of wine, Noddy rested in a corner and Cass scuttered around the sizzling stove.

'Is so frustrating,' said Cass as she turned some meatballs. 'All this food I prepared for the ladies and then it was cancelled, just this afternoon.'

'Some of them are quite old,' replied Kat, 'and you know how cautious they can be when a bad cold is going around.'

'Is no bother, though,' smiled Cass. 'At least we can enjoy it all. Thank you for inviting me. I hope you are hungry.'

'I am. And thirsty. And thanks for cooking – it smells delicious. I don't like to admit it but Greek food is better than Croatian!'

Kat got up and poured them both another glass of wine when suddenly Noddy's head jerked up, ears pricked. His head stayed rigid, eyes fixed on the doorway into the dark living room and a low growl rolled out. Both Kat and Cass turned and paused, and looked at each other fearfully.

'Can you hear anything?' Kat whispered.

'Nothing except the dog and the cooking.'

'Turn everything off, hold onto Noddy's collar, and stay where you are. I'll be back in a second.'

Kat quietly slipped out of another door and came back moments later holding an old rifle and a large Bowie knife.

'My old equipment. Just in case,' she smiled as Cass' eyes opened wide with surprise.

Noddy was continuing to growl as Cass held him. The two women stood still and listened intently. Nothing. And then…the sound of a chair being knocked, somewhere near the back door, the other side of the living room. A sudden ferocious bark from Noddy who leapt up, broke free from Cass and bounded into the darkness. Kat thrust the knife into Cass' hand and ran after Noddy with Cass close behind.

In the darkness of the boot room, the massive form of Noddy had stopped and was barking madly at something that was cowering back into the boot room only feet away. Kat rushed into the room, cocked her rifle and flicked the light switch. She saw a tall lanky man in a black face mask, apparently terrified, squeezing himself against the back wall as Noddy held him there. She recognized him – that man who'd been lurking around the Weir all week.

Blood up, she raised her rifle at him and shouted, 'What the hell are you doing in my house? Tell me now or I'll set my dog on you! Or shoot you! Or both!'

Beside her, Cass looked almost as wild and fierce as she brandished the knife threateningly. The man was motionless, petrified, eyes flitting in fear from one woman to the other and then to the dog, before a fumbling hand found the handle to the back door and, with a loud whimper, opened the door and hurtled out into the darkness. Ordering Noddy to stay, Kat ran out after the man and saw him stumbling through the garden towards the road. She raised her rifle, cursed, and fired a shot over his head.

Inside the Bottom Ship not far away, with only a few days to go until the Spaniards went home, everyone was having a great time. Costumed representatives of the Pantomime Society had just finished another brief promotional scene that somehow ended with a tipsy Captain Hook kissing an equally tipsy Peter Pan, aka Kate from the riding school. Jack as Smee and Tinker Bell were chatting with Dan Williams and enjoying the company of the Spanish boys who'd become good friends. In a corner, Dan's sister Anne was having a quiet and intimate conversation with Teo, Pete and Elisa were laughing together on another table, Mark was there with Ron and Sid, Bill and Vince were propping up the bar and the beers were flowing. And then they heard the shot.

Everyone put down their drinks and rushed outside. In the half light, up the road near Kat's cottage, they heard yelling and could see a figure trying to run away towards the woods.

'That's Kat shouting,' said Vince. 'Sounds like she's in trouble. Come on boys, hurry over to see what's up.'

Without a second invitation, Mark, Dan and Fabio started to sprint up the road with the others not far behind. Within moments they'd reached Kat's cottage where she quickly shouted about a thief, pointing frantically further up where the figure of a tall man was escaping.

The quickest of the group, Mark and Fabio, set off at pace after him but, when they had closed to within 20 metres, they saw that the man had almost reached the deep darkness of the woods. He turned briefly to look backwards at his pursuers then stumbled on the verge, falling heavily onto the grass before trying to scramble back onto his feet.

'He's getting up,' Mark shouted to Fabio as they continued towards him. 'Let's go and get him. You know how to chop tackle, in rugby?'

'I think so,' panted Fabio. 'I watch rugby. Knock his legs away, yes?'

'That'll do.'

They both raced towards the figure that was now on his feet, Mark moving to one side and Fabio to the other. As Bram was almost into the woods, the boys hit him, Fabio diving at his legs while at the same time Mark hurled himself at Bram's chest from the opposite direction. Bram was flipped horizontal and hit the ground hard, Mark's heavy body squashing the breath from his lungs and pinning him helplessly.

'Fabio, go and grab some rope from the pub,' said Mark, sprawled across the squirming victim, 'so we can tie him up. And get someone to call the police.'

Underneath him, Bram wriggled and mumbled something incoherent but Mark just spread his weight a bit more, held down a flailing arm and waited. A concerned crowd including a lumbering Jack and the rest of the panto troupe had come up from the pub as Fabio returned with some old rope which Mark then started using to bind Bram's hands and legs together. The man was still fighting for escape and Mark was having difficulties holding him down.

'Here Jack,' he gasped, 'you're big enough in that fat suit. Sit on his chest, would you? And Hooky, grab his ankles.'

Smee and Captain Hook did as they were bidden as Mark grappled with the flicking rope. Mark, still struggling, turned to Fabio.

115

'Is the constrictor knot right over left,' Mark asked him, 'or left over right? I can never remember.'

With Bram finally tied and pinned securely to the ground, Mark roughly pulled off the face mask. Vince, who'd been watching the scene, suddenly took out his mobile phone and called to the three still on top of the bound man.

'One for the record. Smile, please!'

Once photographs had been taken, Mark and Fabio hauled the culprit to his unsteady feet and marched him back towards the pub. Grazed, bloodied, battered and very bruised, Bram scowled and was silent for most of the way, walking the gauntlet of the abusive and hostile crowds who had come out to watch the drama. Brian, the landlord, had the door of the cellar open, ready to thrust Bram inside and lock the door while waiting for the police to arrive.

'Serves you right,' shouted Sid as Bram passed. 'The rats in there are going to love you!'

'Oi!' cried Brian. 'There's no rats in my cellars, you cheeky beggar. I've a mind to throw you in there too!'

As the door was about to be closed, Bram finally found his voice.

'You're all mad!' he shouted hoarsely. 'You're all in it together! I know the gold is here somewhere. I'll be back, I promise!'

The door slammed shut and was padlocked. Everyone looked at each other and breathed a collective sigh of relief.

Drama over, most went back into the pub while Pete and Elisa went to check on Kat and Cass up the road. Both women were sitting on the wall outside, wine glasses in hand, a new bottle balanced between them, nibbling on cold meze, the rifle and knife hidden in the shadows alongside.

'You okay, Kat?' Pete asked. 'That must have been scary for you.'

'Not really,' Kat smiled back, fully composed. 'It was just a bit of fun. Reminds me of the old times, back in Croatia. I enjoyed having a rifle in my hands again.'

'I liked it too,' said Cass. 'I always have a knife at home, under my bed, in case of troubles. Us Greeks must always be ready and watch out for the Turks. Me and

Kat, we fight together well, don't we, sister?'

They hugged and downed their wines together and Cass reached for the new bottle.

'That man was shouting about some gold before they locked him up,' Pete told them. 'It seems he was looking for some. Nobody at the pub knows what he was talking about. Do you have any idea, Kat?'

'Gold?' asked Kat, perplexed. 'Why should I know about gold? I don't have any, more's the pity. If that man was looking for gold, there's none around here. I think he was just a common thief, looking for anything valuable.'

'He chose the wrong house, that's all,' said Cass. 'No gold, just two angry women who will do the job properly if he shows his face here again.'

Kat fetched two more glasses as Pete and Elisa joined them outside. After a few minutes, two police cars hurried down the road and pulled up sharply at the pub. A crowd welcomed them and Brian opened the cellar to release Bram who was cuffed, bustled briskly into one of the cars and taken away. The other car stayed as statements started to be taken. While the police were distracted, Vince wandered up the road, beer in hand, to join the others on the wall.

'Fun and games over,' he said. 'They'll be up here in a minute to get statements. They did ask a few questions but were keen to get that villain into custody.'

'What questions did they ask?' Kat enquired cautiously.

'Well,' Vince replied. 'They say that someone reported a shot being fired and asked if anybody knew anything about that.'

Kat looked at Pete, worry furrowing her brow.

'Don't worry, Kat,' Vince reassured her. 'Nobody told them about your gun. We all said that the report was mistaken, that it must have been a car backfiring or a door slamming. You'd better hide it again before the cops come. Your secret's safe with us, love.'

Kat slid from the wall and quickly took the rifle and knife inside, stowing them back under the floorboards in her bedroom. She emerged again promptly with yet another bottle of wine.

'Just in case it's a long night,' she smiled, watching the police heading in their direction.

20

Friday afternoon. The Porlock Maria lay anchored in the bay, sails in, rocking steadily in the light swell that slapped the sides. On shore at picturesque Porlock Weir, tourists casually strolled along the harbourside and across the stony beach, enjoying the dying remnants of the summer. On deck, Ramon sat and watched them wistfully, a steaming coffee at his side and a small cigar, his one indulgence, between his fingers.

He'd enjoyed this short break. The ship had been a success, the crew were all in good spirits, the training had progressed well and the people of this small Somerset community had welcomed him and his friends with genuine warm-hearted enthusiasm and affection. It reminded him of his childhood, growing up in a small fishing village in Spain, where everybody knew and looked after everyone else. That village had now disappeared, erased from the land forever by vast concrete creations that lined the shore endlessly, the friendly faces long gone, replaced by faceless commerce. Inevitable progress, a struggling country fighting to survive, yet Ramon's soul pined for the lost ideal. And now here he was, in this quiet unspoiled corner of the world, where the essence of that past life seemed to continue still. His heart had truly warmed to the people of Porlock. He could easily stay for longer but his time was almost up, his business beckoned him home.

Now 58, Ramon knew he'd had a good life. He was wealthy, very wealthy, but he and his family had worked hard for it and, thanks to perseverance and luck through the tougher times, they'd survived and flourished. He was a tough businessman, he'd had to be, and yet generous to his family, friends and those less fortunate. When he'd been approached for the commission of the Porlock Maria and had heard the tale, he'd been overwhelmed at the munificence of the guardians of the gold over the ages, of their determination to help those in need in the community. Although this benevolence had always been conducted furtively, there was no doubt that the spirit of goodwill had seeped into the souls of the people here. Even today, the triathlon last weekend proved that this spirit remained strong. Many of the inhabitants here, whatever their situation, always smiled, always had a joke and always helped each other.

Over the last two weeks, Ramon had become good friends with many of them. His involvement with the Porlock Maria was an honour for him and his family and yet he yearned to do something more for these remarkable people. Something to help them further. As he sat alone and sipped his coffee, he weighed the pros and cons in his mind one last time. It was an idea he'd had several days ago but it was a big decision. He'd spoken to his sister Elisa, the only one he could truly trust, and she'd agreed with him. Some others in his family may not understand but he was at the helm now, it was his money, and it was a legacy that he would be proud of. The decision had been made. He finished his coffee and waited for his two guests to arrive.

Only he knew who they were. He normally met his single contact alone, at night-time, when a discreet rowing boat would make its way to the ship, in the shadows and hopefully unseen. But now, with the Spanish team flying home on Sunday morning and the drama with the South African over, there was less need for secrecy. The crew were busy with the training below, Elisa was on shore somewhere and the deck was quiet. Ramon took a last puff on his cigar and watched the boat, this time with two people in it, rowing steadily out from the harbour. They both needed to hear what he had to say.

Some eyes saw them arrive but it was no matter. If questioned, they'd say they were visiting the crew on the ship one last time. After they had secured the boat and climbed the rope ladder, Ramon welcomed them on board like the close friends they'd become. Sitting on deck, the two waited in anticipation, in the knowledge that Ramon had something important to tell them, something that was hopefully not bad news.

The immediate conversation revolved around the drama of the previous evening, of Bram's arrest and the rumours surrounding the man that had seeped from the initial police reports that morning. Kat and others at Porlock Weir had been visited by the police earlier, to gather more statements and fill them in on the South African. Fingerprint evidence proved that it was Bram who had broken into Molly's house during the triathlon.

His real name was Hans Albert, a known conman and thief who'd travelled under many different guises and was wanted by Interpol. Specialising in the theft of high value antiquities, he'd recently been tracked to Spain where he had been researching lost gold and treasures from the medieval period, before the trail went cold once again. Transported overnight and now securely locked in Bristol Prison, he faced a bleak future. Mark and Fabio were in line for special commendations, it was whispered. All witnesses had agreed to omit any mention of firearms.

The trio sat back, all content with palpable relief at potential disaster averted at the eleventh hour. Reaching below his chair, Ramon pulled out a chilled bottle of champagne and three glasses, handing the glasses out to the grateful others as the cork flew into the sea below.

'To the successful culmination of our venture,' he announced, 'and to the hard work that you have both put in.'

Clinks, sips and smiles before Ramon, putting his glass down on the small table between them, looked from one to the other with more serious intent.

'It is lovely to talk about our success,' he said, 'but this isn't the reason I asked you on board. I have something else to suggest to you, something I have been considering for a while.

'When you first came to me and asked me to build the Porlock Maria, and told me the story of the gold, I was worried. I am a businessman who plays mainly by the rules and the deal sounded suspicious. But, after all of our meetings, I started to understand that we could make it happen, that there was a way to sell you the ship in exchange for the gold - which I still believe belongs to Spain. Okay, the Spanish stole it from the Incas and then the English stole it from the Spanish, so there is no innocent party. You English have spent most of it over the centuries and I think it is only fair that the last of it is returned home. So, we have made it happen. To me, it was just a business deal. But, over the last two weeks, I have been thinking of something else.'

He sat back and took a slow sip of champagne as the others waited in silent trepidation.

'As you know, we will all be leaving you very soon,' Ramon continued eventually, 'and I will personally be very sad about that. All of us, myself included, have had a wonderful time here and we have all grown to love this place and its people. I have made some very good friends in a short time and all of you have genuinely touched my heart. My sister Elisa feels the same. It is a wonderful part of the world and I feel proud that I have helped make the people happy with my ship. And we understand the difficulties in this area, especially for the young and their families trying to find homes. Because of this, I have decided that I would like to help more. I would like you to consider a proposal that I have for you.'

He paused as if gathering his thoughts while the other two listened intently, intrigued.

'I would like to buy the Porlock Maria back from you,' he started.

'Before you ask questions,' he went on as the others stared in surprise, 'please let me explain.

'The Porlock Maria is a beautiful ship, maybe the best that we have made, and I will be sorry to see her go although I know that she is in the best possible care. So…I propose that I buy her back but let you and the people here keep her on permanent loan forever.'

The others, shocked almost into silence, looked at Ramon as he paused to check if they'd heard right.

'So,' said T slowly, 'if I understand correctly, we keep the ship and go ahead with the plans we have for it, and you will return the gold to us as payment?'

'No,' replied Ramon. 'It will be easier than that. The gold is already in my vault in Spain where it will remain and where it belongs. It is a part of my country's heritage, from a time when we were trading materials for gold in Africa, although those times are dark. Instead, I am happy to send you the market value of the gold in sterling, to a local bank account that I have already set up with the help of a solicitor here, and I will say that the money is an extra donation from me. My finance people can make this happen with no questions asked, and this will also protect you and your identities as the guardians of the gold forever.'

'But that will cost you a fortune,' said M, incredulous. 'Everyone here thinks you've already paid for the ship yourself and now you're donating the same amount again?'

'I am a wealthy man,' Ramon replied. 'I know that the people of Porlock need that money more than I do. Yes, you have the ship but you also need money to improve your lives in other ways as well.'

He looked at the two carefully before a wry smile spread across his face.

T was the first to catch on. 'So Ramon…I think you have a plan?'

'I do,' said Ramon, 'a plan and a proposal. I hope you like what I have to say.'

The three sat around the table, enjoyed more champagne, and discussed. By the time the bottle had been finished, the proposal had been laid out in fine detail and accepted in its entirety by the guardians. Initially they had difficulty understanding the details of the new venture, all the financial, legal and local angles, but Ramon had all the answers and the plan seemed solid.

'My solicitor here knows all the details and can be trusted,' Ramon said as they were finishing off. 'He has also started to speak to the other party, as we discussed, and so we can move as quickly as we want. So…are we all in agreement?'

'I think we are,' replied T, gratefully shaking Ramon's hand. 'We'll need to tell Fan, the other guardian, but I'm sure it'll be okay.'

With that, the two clambered carefully back down to their boat and started back towards shore.

'I'm stunned by the generosity of the man,' said T as M pulled skilfully towards the harbour. 'I mean, first the ship and then this. What on earth will everyone make of it?'

'No idea,' replied M, straining but making quick headway. 'But at least that South African, Hans wossisname, is out of the picture now. That would have added more complications.'

'Yes, we're lucky he went. I was dreading having to get rid of him. We were right about him all along, just a chancer, a conman, a thief.'

'And if he tells someone about the gold,' said M, 'nobody will believe him as it's disappeared. With Ramon's help, our tracks have been covered. I think we're in the clear.'

'Let's hope so,' replied T. 'I'll send a message to Fan tonight about Ramon's plan. By the way, I forgot to tell you that I asked Fan about Rik's death, whether it was connected to the secret. I just want to clear up all the questions before our merry troupe is disbanded forever.'

'And?'

'The reply was that his death was completely unrelated. Just a genuine accident after all, as we thought.'

'Or,' pondered M, 'what if Rik was killed because he knew something and Fan was responsible, and just doesn't want to tell us?'

'No, it doesn't work like that. We're all in it together, all three of us. No secrets between us all. If one of us falls, we all fall. Fan can be trusted. If he, or she, says that Rik's death was nothing to do with all of this, it's true.'

'Well, that's a relief. I'm too told to go to prison if it was anything else. A huge weight off my mind.'

'And mine,' replied T. 'And, if Rik's death was anything to do with the guardians and it came out, then the Porlock Maria venture would be blown out of the water too, so to speak.'

'You're right,' replied M. 'Tongues were wagging but they've stopped now, thank God.'

'And you're sure you told Ramon only about the history of the gold and the donations over the years? Nothing of the…darker side of our responsibility?'

'Don't worry,' M said. 'I told him only what he needed to know, as we agreed. Some secrets have to stay secret.'

'Good,' replied T as M approached the harbour. 'Our story is nearly at its end. Only one or two more surprises, I feel, before we can all rest at last.'

'What do you mean?' asked M.

'The end of one story and the start of many others,' replied T cryptically. 'Tomorrow is going to be a big day.'

T paused and looked hesitant before taking a deep breath and announcing, ''There's one more thing I need to tell you, while we're alone.'

'Oh, yes?' M replied.

'I need to tell somebody who I am, that I am a guardian. It's someone I can trust

completely who will never tell another soul. I know we agreed never to tell anybody else but, once I tell you why, I hope you'll understand.'

And, before they finally reached the jetty, T told M a short story, of death and love and the future. As they tied up the boat, M understood.

21

Friday evening and the sun was appearing intermittently from behind the high clouds that swam leisurely east. The last warmth of the day was slowly dissipating as Pete and Elisa sat on a bench at Porlock Weir, beers in hand, looking out across the harbour towards the ship and the expanse of sea. Elisa took his left hand and held it aloft, allowing the sun to glint through the ruby in Pete's ring and tinge his forehead with a warm red glow. She turned to him, smiling softly.

'I think your ring has made its spell,' she said. 'The legend could be true. I mean, it has drawn us together and look at us now.'

Pete looked at his ring, took it off and gently slipped it onto Elisa's finger.

'For you to keep now, my love,' he said. 'A gift from me to you. And it suits you better too.'

'Are you sure?' she smiled.

'Of course. I checked with Mum and she's happy for you to have it too. She told me that she thinks the charm has worked for me and also may have worked for her.'

'And has it?'

'You know, Elisa, I think it has. I don't really believe in superstition but Mum and Seb – well, they've become very close, as you know. Mum told me that she was starting to feel her age, getting a bit despondent and tired, but she says she has a new lease of life now.'

'I am so glad for her, and thank you for the ring,' Elisa replied, taking Pete's hand. 'It is very special.'

'But tell me,' she continued, 'does Eve still want to come with us on Sunday? I talked to Seb and he still wants her to come.'

'I saw her earlier and, yes, she's made up her mind. She says that if I can have more adventures, then so can she. Never say die, she said. She's got a wild spirit, just like me, I suppose. She said that, even though she's about seven years older than Seb, she's always wanted a toy boy. I know, it sounds ridiculous but I'm behind her all the way. She's happy.'

'And Pete,' said Elisa quietly, 'what about you. Do you still want to come? You sure you want to do this? It is a big change for you and we've only known each other a short time.'

Pete looked into her dark eyes and kissed her. 'I've never been more sure of anything.'

'You will not miss your friends here and the land of your home?'

Pete looked out at the calm sea. 'A lot of my friends have moved on, one way or another, and I've always had a restless soul, wanting more adventures. I'll miss Porlock but I can always visit whenever I want. I was staying here to look after Mum but I don't need to worry about that any more. It might sound strange but I think I'm on the verge of finding true happiness, true love, for the first time ever.'

'Love?' Elisa replied coyly, a twinkle in her eye.

'Yes, Elisa,' he said, smiling back at her. 'That funny feeling that churns your stomach, lifts your heart and fills your every moment with an overwhelming desire to see that one person, to talk to her, to hold her, to kiss her. Yes, it feels like love to me.'

'So no more Mister Prowler?'

'Those days are over now, I promise. I feel as if I've been waiting for you my whole life and, now you're here, I don't want to let you go. I'll stay by your side for as long as you want me. If you'll still have me?'

'I think, Peter my love, that I will. My heart is lifted too and my stomach is warm. I like your face and I like kissing it, and I like hugging you. I am not very romantic but, for me, I think this could be the beginnings of love too.'

He kissed her smiling face once again and then, raising her hand, kissed the ring. They sat in contented silence, looking out over the sea, hand in hand, for several minutes before Pete made moves to stand.

'I'd love to spend all afternoon here,' he said wistfully, 'but I need to go and see Kat. She's my best friend and I need to tell her first.'

'Of course, Pete, you must go. Kat is a good woman and a good friend. She will understand, I am sure of it.'

Another embrace and promises to meet up later, before Pete sauntered off towards the old cottage leaving Elisa alone on the bench, watching the ship and pondering the strange events of the last two weeks in this wonderful land. The sun shone down on her and she allowed her heart to soar.

***

They sat outside in the small garden as the shadows lengthened, Noddy stretched out on the rough lawn, snoring contentedly. Kat fetched them both cold bottles of beer and sat down at the weather-beaten iron table opposite Pete, watching him with interest. His face was set, the usual casual smile missing and he was unusually quiet.

'Well, old friend, what is it?' she asked to break the deadlock. 'Something is up. I know you - you have something on your mind.'

'You're right,' he admitted. 'I do have something to tell you. Well, a few things. It's not easy for me. I'm not sure where to start.'

'Just open your mouth and the words will come out. You can tell me anything, you know that.'

'Thanks, Kat,' he smiled. 'But you may not like everything I have to say.'

'Let me judge that. Please, go ahead and tell me what's on your mind.'

And so Pete, deciding to plunge straight in, took a deep breath and told her about Elisa and their plans. Not only that he was going to go to Spain, possibly forever, but that Eve was also going to go with Seb, for new loves, new lands, and new adventures.

'I'm glad for you, Pete,' said Kat, wiping away a tear as he finished, 'and I am not surprised. You've been acting out of character for the last few days and I guessed something like this was going to happen. Elisa's a lovely woman and you two go well together.'

'It wasn't an easy decision,' Pete replied, 'leaving Porlock, my friends – and you.'

'Oh, don't worry about me,' she smiled bravely. 'I can look after myself, you know that. Just come back and see me sometime, that's all I ask. I'll miss you.'

'I'll miss you too, very much. But I feel that it's the right thing to do, for me. And it's good for Mum too.'

They took another swig of beer and a brief silence descended between them.

'You said you had a few things to tell me,' asked Kat. 'Was there anything else?'

'Yes, there is something,' Pete admitted. He paused. 'It's about Will.'

'Oh, yes?'

'I need to tell you something about him, Kat. He was my close friend and he told me things, some of which you probably already know. But there is something else.'

Kat froze, anguish and memories still raw after only five short years since his disappearance. Eyes wide, face pale and mouth slightly open in worried anticipation. She remained silent, staring, waiting for the news.

'Before I go on,' Pete continued, 'I must ask you not to repeat what I have to say to any living soul, ever. Not to Mark, not to your friends, nobody. Please, it's very important.'

Kat paused and took a deep breath. 'I promise, Pete.'

Pete paused to collect his thoughts. 'There is something that you didn't know about Will. You once told me that you sensed that Will was hiding something from you but you never knew what.'

'Yes, that's true. I asked him several times but he just told me it was the money worries, that's all.'

'Well, Kat, it was something else. It's a long and strange tale that Will and me were involved in. Don't worry, it's nothing bad. It's just a very old secret that must still remain a secret, which is why I asked you never to repeat this. You might not believe it but, as I sit here, Kat, I swear that all of it is true.'

Kat sat back, intrigued and confused, and waited for Pete to tell his tale.

And so Pete weaved a wonderful saga, of ancient battles, stolen Spanish gold and smuggling, of the Donna Maria, of legacy, death and joy through the ages, and of the ghosts. He told of the ancient promise to use the gold for the people, of absolute secrecy and loyalty. He told of the three trusted guardians who remained true to the old vow, the two who worked together and the third who was never known, who would protect the secret and punish corruption by whatever means necessary. He told of the ending of the story, of the Porlock Maria, the last of the gold and of a ruthless thief who sought it but failed. A tale of intrigue, secrecy and deception, to alleviate hardship and spread happiness to the people of a small corner of Somerset. A history that will never be known.

'I can scarcely believe it,' Kat said when Pete had finished. 'Such a strange tale. I mean, you hear rumours all the time, about anonymous requests for help with odd things, and we know about the donations over the years, but I had no idea about all this. It's difficult to take in.'

'All true,' admitted Pete, 'which is why I swore you to secrecy. I thought you needed to know before I go.'

'But you said that Will was involved? He never told me anything about this, I'm sure of it. And how do you know all of this anyway?'

'Ah, that's the last part of the story that I need to tell you,' Pete replied tentatively.

'Will had a good heart, as you know. He always wanted to help others and put himself second. Many years ago, soon after you'd both come to Porlock with Mark, Will was recruited as one of the guardians. His code name was Mas. He helped look after and distribute the gold but, of course, never used any for himself even though you had money worries. And, before you ask, I can promise you that his death was nothing to do with any of this.'

'How do you know all of this?' Kat asked again.

'Because I was – I am – another of the guardians. I was the one who recruited Will in the first place, as I knew his family had lived here for generations and I knew he could be trusted. When he died, there were rumours of foul play, even suicide, but it wasn't like that, I swear. It was just a horrible accident, Kat.'

Kat wiped away a few tears and was silent for a few moments, looking over Pete's shoulder into the garden beyond.

'I should be furious with you, Pete,' she began emotionally, 'for not telling me earlier. You're my best friend. I should have known about all this. You should have told me.'

'I'm so sorry, Kat, I truly am. But I was bound by an oath of strict secrecy, and I still am. Will was the same – he couldn't tell you although I'm sure he wanted to. The only reason I'm telling you now is that all of this is now over. And I'm leaving. And you need to know the truth.'

'But you deceived me. You could have trusted me, you know that.'

'Believe me, I've wanted to tell you, so much. The secrecy, the deception, the fear of discovery, everything, has been eating at me constantly. I'm not proud of it all but I took an oath. To keep the secret and help the people of Porlock. I admit I have my faults and I'm not looking for forgiveness. Just maybe a bit of understanding.'

'I think I understand,' Kat said after a brief pause, 'but it's still hard to take in. I thought Will and I had no secrets.'

'I'm sorry, Kat,' Pete said again. 'I wish it could have been different but at least now you know.'

'So,' Kat went on, gathering her thoughts after a deep breath, 'what is your code name, Pete?'

'My name is Tas. We've always used code names when we communicate to protect our identities, in case one of us slips up and reveals our real names. When all of this began, in 1668, it was decided that the three guardians would be called Fan, Tas and Mas, from the Spanish word for ghosts, Fantasmas. Due to the Spanish connection and the fact that we'd have to exist like ghosts, invisible to everybody else.'

'So if Will was Mas, who replaced him when he disappeared?'

'Bob is Mas now. You know, Bob the Box with the boat.'

'Bob? Well, I would never have guessed that! My, it's been a very strange couple of weeks.'

'You're right there,' Pete replied. 'Possibly the strangest couple of weeks of my life.'

'You're a dark horse, Pete,' Kat smiled. 'You've got hidden and interesting depths and a kind soul. I should have taken up that offer of marriage. Elisa's a lucky woman.'

'Thanks, Kat. If it doesn't work out, I'll be back and I'll look you up.'

'You better do, handsome. By the way, you said Ramon knew what was happening but does Elisa too?'

'No, she knows a bit but not the whole story. Ramon promised not to tell anybody else.'

'So are you going to tell her?'

'Maybe,' Pete replied, 'I'll get to know her better first but I think I can trust her. I've only known her for two weeks, after all.'

They finished their second beer and Pete stood, preparing to leave. The two hugged as friends and Pete moved towards the door.

'One last thing, Pete,' Kat said, holding open the door. 'If you are Tas and Bob is Mas, who is Fan?'

Pete kissed her on the cheek. 'I have no idea, my love. Now it's all over, we may never know.'

22

On Saturday afternoon, almost exactly two weeks after the Porlock Maria had arrived, the podium and speakers were set up in the same position at Porlock Weir. The crowds were larger than previously, all murmuring in contented anticipation of what Ramon would say. This was the last full day before the Spaniards flew home, leaving the ship in capable and well-drilled hands. Salty, the new captain, had confirmed that he was happy with the new crew. Everything had gone to plan. Ramon had arranged a farewell gathering by the harbour, attended by several hundred locals, dozens of new friends and a scatter of curious tourists.

At two o'clock precisely, Ramon, this time dressed informally in light chinos and a polo shirt and flanked by Elisa, Seb, Cass and most of the Spanish crew, stepped up and turned on the microphone. A ripple of quiet moved through the crowd and they all turned in anticipation to watch and listen.

'Our friends!' Ramon began, raising his arms and beaming widely. 'We can call you that now, I hope.'

Cheers, whistling, applause and enthusiastic yells from all sides confirmed that the Spanish had truly been taken to heart by this small community. When the cacophony subsided, Ramon scanned the audience and continued.

'As you know, we are leaving tomorrow, flying back to Spain. We will be very sad to go. We have all had a wonderful two weeks here and we wish we could stay longer. But it is not possible. Before we go, however, I must tell you all something very important.'

He paused, cleared his throat and, looking around the hushed crowd slowly once more, adopted a serious expression.

'I have been in discussion with my accountants over the last few days and there is a complication. My family's donation of that wonderful ship that you see in the bay, the Porlock Maria, to the people of Porlock is causing a few tax problems, I am very sorry to say. I will not go into details but, to be brief, I am no longer permitted to give you the ship.'

An audible gasp and flutters of mutterings swept through the incredulous crowd. Before the noise increased, though, Ramon continued.

'But,' he boomed, quietening the hubbub, 'it is not all bad news. I and my family have decided that, although we still need to be the owners of the ship, we will let the people here have it on permanent loan forever so that it can fulfil the destiny it was built for. To help the people of Porlock. I will of course need to charge a bit of rent for it – one pint of Exmoor beer when I return every year to see my old friends!'

A growing and excited clamour from the crowd before Ramon quickly raised his arms to quieten them again.

'There is one more thing,' he announced. 'My friends from Spain and I have all grown to love the people here and we understand that times are difficult for some. Especially the young men and women who need homes to raise their families. This is one of the reasons why the Porlock Maria came. We are unfortunately not able to give you the ship anymore and so we have decided to give you something else instead.

'There is a new development of houses being built on the edge of the village and they will be finished soon. I have been in negotiation with the developer and solicitors here and we have come to an arrangement. My family has decided to buy the whole development, eight houses in total. It has been agreed that all the houses will be rented exclusively to young families of this area who have no place of their own, as starter homes. The rent will be only nominal. The houses can be occupied by the same family for no more than five years, to help them find their feet, before the houses will be passed on to other young families who need them. All this will be managed by a local agent. I signed the paperwork this morning.'

This time, there was no stopping them. Before Ramon had an opportunity to say much more, they cascaded noisily across the footbridge to swamp the Spanish troupe who disappeared among the throng of thankful well-wishers. For those who remained on the near side of the harbour, the clamour of excited chatter was all that could be heard.

On the stony beach to one side stood Joe, Colin and Bob and, not far away, the more austere and reflective farmers' gathering of Vic, George, Raymond and Jack, with Jack's wife Laura and baby Samantha sitting idly on a nearby bench. As soon as Ramon had made his announcement, the farmers huddled together in muted conversation, away from any prying ears. Joe was watching them.

He wandered off towards the other group of men and, after a brief discussion, returned with the others following slowly behind.

'Bob, Colin,' Joe began when they had all assembled. 'These boys have something to tell you.'

It was Vic who opened. 'Joe told us about the rumours going around,' he said, looking pointedly at Colin, 'about one of us being the anonymous person who sometimes asks people for help with local good causes.'

'Well, it was just an idea I had,' blustered Colin. 'I mean, it was just idle speculation, Vic.'

'That's okay,' Vic continued. 'We all know about the strange requests over the years and it makes sense that they could come from someone in one of the established Exmoor families. Joe said you thought it may be Raymond here. But I have to tell you, it wasn't any of us.'

'You told Joe you'd overheard a private meeting we'd had up at Vic's farm,' chipped in Jack. 'Well, we were discussing something to do with the future of Porlock.'

'We may as well tell them, lads,' said George. 'I mean, after what the Spaniard has just said, we've agreed that our idea is redundant now, isn't it?'

'It is,' Vic replied. 'You see, Colin, for several weeks we've been having talks with property developers who were interested in buying up some farmland for housing. We all know about the housing crisis for the youngsters and we all felt that we should do what we can to help. It wasn't about the money, it was about the community. We didn't want to make our discussions public because of the potential outcry.'

'But,' continued Jack, 'it looks like we don't have to worry about it anymore, thank God. And thanks to Ramon too. We did mention the situation to him in passing and he must have realised how critical it was and decided to help.'

'I can't believe his generosity, though,' said George. 'I mean, it must be costing him a couple of million at least. And the cost of the ship too.'

'He is extremely generous,' agreed Vic, 'and also very wealthy. A good man.'

'It's very generous of all of you as well,' said Colin. 'Even to consider selling off some of your land, your livelihoods, to help others.'

'It's what we've always done,' said George. 'Our fathers and their fathers before them, we've always helped out as best we could. This is Exmoor – we help each other.'

'But,' Colin continued, considering, 'I have to ask. This anonymous person who asks us to help out, to help the community. If it's not any of you lot, then who is it? You must have some idea.'

They all shook their heads in genuine bafflement.

'No idea,' said Jack finally. 'But, if I did know, I'd shake his hand.'

***

Kat and Pete stood alone on the beach close to the cottage, watching the crowds milling about by the harbour and still eager to talk to Ramon, Elisa and the others. Without him scarcely noticing, she took Pete's hand and gave it an affectionate squeeze.

'I don't know what to say, Pete,' she said, turning towards him, 'I really don't. Mark told me a short while ago.'

'Well,' Pete replied, 'I'm going away, possibly for a long time. I don't need the house anymore and I couldn't be bothered to get it sold through an agent. And I don't need the money – I've got enough in the bank to keep me happy.'

'But to give your house to Mark and Beth, just like that! It's more than generous. You're a true Godsend. Words fail me.'

'Mark, Beth and Amy need a house and I have one spare – simple. They won't have to worry about the rent anymore and it'll give them the security they need. When Mark's away on the ship, Beth won't need to worry so much about getting a job.'

'But it's such a risk. I mean, what if it doesn't work out with you and Elisa?'

'Then I'll think of something else,' Pete replied. 'Do more travelling, maybe. But it will work out with Elisa, I just know.'

'And what about Eve?' Kat asked. 'It's risky with her and Seb too. If that doesn't work, what will she do?'

'She's agreed with me about the house. She said she's not planning to return here, whatever happens. Her and Seb have become quite an item, you know.'

136

Kat gave him a kiss on the cheek. 'I'm going to miss you, Pete. Really miss you. Everything's going to change now, with you gone and Mark sailing to pastures new, literally. I'll still be here for Mark when he needs me and I'll still be here for you too, whenever you come back. I'll carry on and hopefully someday have my own bakery here in the Weir.'

'Oh, yes,' said Pete suddenly, 'I'm glad you reminded me.'

Reaching into his pocket, he brought out something which he placed into Kat's palm.

'That's for you, Kat,' he said, 'to help you start the bakery.'

She looked down, opened her palm and saw a large dulled gold coin engraved with a cross and other symbols, roughly struck and clearly old. She looked back up at Pete, frowning in questioning surprise.

'It's one of the last of the coins from the hoard,' he explained. 'Every guardian was allowed to keep one, as a souvenir, memento or whatever. I don't need it Kat and I thought it might help you. It's very rare, worth a few thousand.'

'Thank you so much,' she gasped. 'But I don't deserve this. Why are you doing this for me?'

'Guilt, possibly,' Pete replied, 'for not telling you about Will earlier. But also, Kat, you're my best friend. I love you dearly and want you to stay in the place you love and be happy. This will, I hope, help.'

Tears in her eyes, they hugged and in silence watched the cheerful celebrations by the harbour and the Porlock Maria, the harbinger of hope for the future, rocking majestically out in the bay.

***

The evening sun was setting and the moon was slowly rising from behind the hills.

The farewell party in the Bottom Ship that had started early was in boisterous full swing, music thumping out, the outside tables all full, dancing, drinking, promises of eternal friendships, an evening of love and laughter. Eve was there with her elderly friends, all incredulous at her decision yet secretly jealous; Cass was fending off an amorous and persistent local while getting raucously drunk with Kat; Anne and Teo were smooching in a corner, oblivious to everyone else; the other Spanish boys were enjoying the attentions of besotted local girls; Mark and his friends were celebrating, and everyone else was having a joyous time. Nobody was going to miss this send-off.

Outside, on the harbour wall with legs dangling, sat Pete and Bob.

'So it's all come to an end at last,' said Bob, gazing out to sea. 'The pact and the secret that has lasted for over three centuries.'

'And it's ended like this,' mused Pete. 'It's incredible, if you think about it. I mean, the Porlock Maria, the South African, everyone happy. I'm off for new adventures too, unexpectedly.'

'You've told Kat about everything but, apart from her, nobody else knows who we are?'

'Yup. We're still ghosts.'

'But,' said Bob after a pause, 'we still don't know who Fan is. Any ideas?'

Pete gazed out to sea. 'Not really', he said. 'If it wasn't for the notes, I'd put it all down to imagination. I mean, how can anybody stay undetected for so long, especially by us? I thought we'd be able to find out somehow. No, it's a mystery. Fan is the real ghost here.'

'Maybe it's good that we don't know,' Bob replied quietly. 'The secret's stayed safe and everything has worked out well. Let's leave it like that.'

From behind them, a bellow from Jack. 'There they are! Come on, boys, come and join the party!'

Bob and Pete turned and slid carefully off the harbour wall to be welcomed by the cheerful farming posse of Raymond, Jack, George and Vic, all down from the moor for the party, all holding pints and not all steady on their feet. Jack was also holding a newspaper.

'Have you seen this?' he asked them joyfully. 'Front page of the local rag. The headline says 'Hook Nabs Crook'. Love it! I must get this framed.'

Pete took the paper from Jack and read it, smiling all the time. There they were, the bulky Mark, the flamboyant Captain Hook and the rotund Smee, all sitting and grinning, arms around each other, and, underneath, a grimacing Bram.

'You did well, Jack,' Pete said, 'we all did. Getting rid of that thieving so-and-so. More promotion for the village and great publicity for the panto as well. I need another pint to celebrate, I think.'

'It's your last night, Pete,' slurred Raymond. 'Time to come and have some fun. Elisa's in there and so is everyone else. Come in for the farewell knees-up!'

Without more encouragement, Bob and Pete joined the group and wandered slowly back towards the busy pub, happy to be led back into the fold of their lifelong friends.

'You're going to miss this, Pete,' said Jack, putting an affectionate arm around his shoulder as they walked, lagging behind the others. 'And we're going to miss you too.'

'I will miss you all,' admitted Pete, 'but I'll be back, I promise. Just to keep an eye on you all, make sure you're not getting into any mischief.'

Jack laughed. 'Not possible. But it won't be the same without you here. We've had some fun, eh? If only they knew.'

***

The sun slowly set across the bay as the party continued well into the night. The music eventually died, the last revellers wobbled homewards with loud laughter-filled banter, the taxis had all gone and the lights of the Bottom Ship were finally turned off.

A light breeze rippled the silvered sea under the pale half-moon. The silhouette of the galleon swayed gently in the bay, its dim lamps glinting silently through the darkness. Wrapped in her black shawl and standing alone on the shore, Kat watched, her face set like stone.

The whispers were quieter tonight, the ghosts were asleep. Her thoughts turned to timeless tales of love, death, magic, gold and hope. Her instincts had been true – something had come, something that will change the land here forever.

A flutter from above. She looked up and watched the cap still there, still aloft. But, although she had accepted that Will would never return, a tiny glimmer of golden hope lingered. Her heart was no longer straining, the demons had settled, her vigil was over. Noddy was sitting quietly by her side. She ruffled his huge head, looked up at the moon and smiled.

Epilogue

Many years later, the snow still swirled and the icy wind still whistled and bit.

The children, enraptured, sat in silence by the fire that had reduced to a warming glow. The old man paused and sipped his whisky, his lively eyes flickering behind his glasses. His wife and daughter were on the sofa nearby, both also captivated by the tale. They'd heard it before and yet, although the story always reflected the reality so many years earlier, details often changed at the old man's whim. He preferred to relive the memories in the form of a spooky fairy tale for the children, something that they always enjoy.

'What happened next, Grandad?' asked the little boy.

The old man gathered his thoughts for the ending.

'So, children, one dark night, the wicked pirate went looking for the gold. The wizard, ghosts, the king and the princess were all waiting in the shadows for him. They all surprised him and there was a terrible fight. Eventually, the wizard and the king jumped on the wicked pirate and tied him up. They then sent him to the deepest darkest dungeon where he stayed until he died.

'For helping out, the wizard wanted to reward the two ghosts. They had once been princes who had promised to help protect the land even after they had died. The wizard knew this and so he cast a powerful spell and turned the two ghosts back into handsome young princes.

'One prince had a red ruby ring which he offered to the beautiful princess, giving her a small kiss on the cheek. The princess fell in love with him and they were married by the king with a big celebration at Porlock Weir. And everyone lived happily ever after.'

The children sat happily, smiling up at the old man who smiled back and reached again for his whisky.

'Come on, kids,' said Sam, their mother, rising from the sofa. 'Time for bed now. If you can sleep after that scary story.'

'Grandad?' asked the little boy, ignoring his mother. 'Did that really all happen at Porlock Weir?'

'Oh yes,' replied the old man, a twinkle in his eye. 'At least most of it did. It was a long time ago and there were real ghosts and wizards back then.'

'How do you know?' asked the little girl. 'Were you there?'

'I was,' he replied. 'It was about 40 years ago, when your mummy was very little.'

They looked a little sceptical.

'If you don't believe me,' he continued mildly, 'look over there on the wall.'

They turned to where he was pointing and saw a framed newspaper cutting. Now much faded but the image still clear, they saw Captain Hook, Smee and another sitting proudly on a captured villain. Both children opened their mouths in awe.

'So what was the name of the handsome prince, then?' the boy asked, turning back to his grandfather.

'His name was Peter.'

'That's my name!' shrieked the boy.

'And what about the princess?' asked the girl hopefully. 'What was she called?'

'She came from a land far away and so she had a name that was difficult to pronounce. But it sounds a bit like yours and so let's call her Elisabeth.'

'Come on, children,' said their mother once again. 'It really is time for bed now. If you have any more questions, ask Grandad in the morning.'

And with that, Sam ushered the two excitable children up the stairs and finally to bed, leaving the old man and his wife alone by the fire.

'I love that story,' said Laura when all was quiet. 'Especially that you always pretend that you were a wizard. Or were you one of the ghosts?'

'Either or both, my love,' replied Jack reflectively. 'A bit of fun and fancy, that's all. I think the kids enjoyed the story.'

'I did too. I can't remember – did you ever hear from Pete?'

'Yes, a few times after he left. He stayed in Spain with Elisa until he died, quite a few years ago now.'

'And you told him everything? And Bob too?'

'Yes, I told them both. And that my Dad was Fan before me. They weren't too surprised – I think they might have suspected.'

'And did you ever tell them about the others?' she asked. 'You know, Vic, Raymond and George?'

'Yes. I thought they deserved to know. The community was so tight back then, especially up here on the moor. I told them that I was Fan, the one who was ultimately responsible, but that the others also knew and helped me out when needed. The secret was safe with them – nobody talked. They were good men. All gone now, of course.'

'Bob died a while ago too,' said Laura, 'and so it's just our secret now. Nobody will ever know.'

'Looking back,' said Jack wistfully, 'it is a strange tale. Once we're gone, the only memory of those days as a guardian will be a fairy story that the grandchildren might remember and pass on to their children.'

Laura rose from the sofa, went over towards Jack and gave him a loving kiss on his forehead.

'You're a good man, Jack Court,' she said with affection. 'I've always loved you. They were good times back then.'

'They were,' he agreed, taking her hand. 'And this is the only memory.'

He tapped lightly on a small wooden box on the table by his whisky glass. Inscribed on the top were the words 'For Porlock.'

'You were great at woodworking back then, Jack,' Laura said. 'I've always loved that box.'

'I sent Pete and Bob one too. For the memory.'

Laura opened the box and took out the single dulled and ancient gold coin.

'Something for the grandchildren,' Jack said, finishing his whisky.

Outside, the wind whistled and puffed a few more wisps of smoke down the chimney into the old farmhouse room. Jack smiled and gently blew, and they were gone.

The Legend of the Donna Maria

Partly adapted from 'The Wreck of the Donna Maria' by Derek Purvis

The middle few decades of the 17th century were arguably some of the most volatile and formative years in the history of England. The English Civil War had ended in 1649 with the death of Charles I and Cromwell's Protectorate ruled the country until the restoration of the monarchy in 1660.

Abroad, South America had been invaded and dominated by the Spanish and Portuguese since the 15th century. In the 17th century, North America started to become colonised, primarily by the English and Dutch. The sugar and tobacco plantations of the Caribbean and east coast of America grew quickly, fuelling opportunism for enterprising entrepreneurs. Fortunes were there to be made and many European countries took advantage. The triangular trade, as it was known, was very lucrative - goods manufactured in England and Europe (eg. textiles, tools, firearms) were shipped to Africa, exchanged for slaves, who were then sold in the West Indies and North America, and goods bought there (eg. sugar, cotton, tobacco) were shipped back to Europe for sale. The main European nations involved were Portugal, England, Spain, France, Netherlands and Denmark.

In the 1660s, this was also a time of conflict and tension in Europe. The first Anglo-Dutch War (1652-54) and the Anglo-Spanish War (1654-60), due to commercial rivalry over the colonisation, were recently over. It was no surprise that there was no love lost between the competing trading nations. In England, the west coast was exceptionally busy with the proliferation of trade operating out of Bristol, the main port serving the Americas. The settlements of West Somerset, including Minehead and Porlock, took advantage of this, supplying ships with materials and food (primarily salted beef, sheep and fish) for their arduous journeys ahead. This was also a time when smuggling was rife along the coast, taxes being extremely high, especially for imported goods, to pay for recent expensive wars against the Irish, Dutch and Spanish.

In Porlock at this time, the Rogers family were beef traders and established the tannery there. Rogers himself was also the master of a small supply ship serving those crossing the Atlantic and he also part-owned a larger vessel, the Mary Fortune. Fully aware of how much money could be made in the triangular trade, Rogers, along with a few other local men, decided to get in on the action. As all official trading ships had to register with the authorities, Rogers and his friends decided to sail unofficially, to avoid the high taxes. In 1668, they set sail in the Mary Fortune, captained by Rogers, and headed south.

They stopped off in the port of Santa Cruz in Tenerife, off the west coast of Africa. Santa Cruz was one of the most popular stop-over locations for European traders and, when Rogers arrived, other ships from England, France, Spain, Portugal and the Netherlands were also resting there. As was not unusual, the sailors from all countries were drinking hard and the English sailors quickly got drunk. No doubt spurred on by rivalries and recent hostilities, they started a fight. The fight soon escalated to serious conflict, leading to the whole of the Spanish fleet being burned and the French ships fleeing. The English, despite the loss of four ships, won. They plundered the Spanish ships and amassed a huge fortune in gold, one of the main international currencies of the day, that the Spanish were bringing back from their South American colonies and other trading.

Rogers and his friends grabbed as much gold as they could. The Mary Fortune had been badly damaged in the fighting and so they captured a defeated Portuguese ship, the Donna Maria. In possession of a substantial and unexpected bounty, they decided to return to England.

As they sailed home, they devised a plan. As they were trading illegally, they couldn't land at a major port as, not only were there taxes to consider, they would lose all the gold. And so, knowing the Exmoor coast well, they ran the ship aground on the rugged beach at Glenthorne, just down the coast from Porlock Weir, and made it look like a shipwreck. The crew of about 25 unshipped the gold which was then hidden. The crew were promised a share of the gold once things had quietened down.

Over the next months, some of the gold was used as discreetly as possible, some to buy land and property. Eventually, however, gossip alerted the authorities who came to the area and started searching. The hamlet of Blackford, between Minehead and Porlock, was ransacked; the manor house at Allerford close by was demolished; and Court Place in Porlock was also torn down. Some of Rogers' crew were caught and hanged at Taunton although Rogers himself evaded capture. Despite all this, nobody talked.

What remained of the fortune in gold was never found. Whether it was all used or whether it remains hidden, we will never know. The mystery continues to this very day.

Printed in Dunstable, United Kingdom